MAPS AND SHADOWS

Maps and Shadows

A Novel

by **Krysia Jopek**

AQUILA POLONICA (U.S.) LTD.
10850 Wilshire Boulevard, Suite 300, Los Angeles, California 90024, U.S.A.
www.AquilaPolonica.com

Published in both hardcover and trade paperback 2010.
eBook edition published 2013.

ISBN (cloth): 978-1-60772-007-2
20 19 18 17 16 15 14 13 12 11 10   1 2 3 4 5 6 7 8 9 10

ISBN (trade paperback): 978-1-60772-008-9
20 19 18 17   2 3 4 5 6 7 8 9 10

ISBN (eBook): 978-1-60772-013-3

Printed in the U.S.A.

Library of Congress Control Number 2010931249

Acknowledgments:

Cover design by Stefan Mucha based on an original concept by Lou Robinson. Photographs and other illustrative material are reproduced with permission, and are from the collections of Henry Jopeck, Stefan Mucha and Helen Zasada. Author photo by Shana Sureck.

For Henry, Helen and Joseph,
and in memory of Zofia and Andrzej

THE CARTOGRAPHER,
BUSY REARRANGING BORDERS,

DOES NOT HEAR THE GUNSHOTS,
GLIMPSE THE PEOPLE...

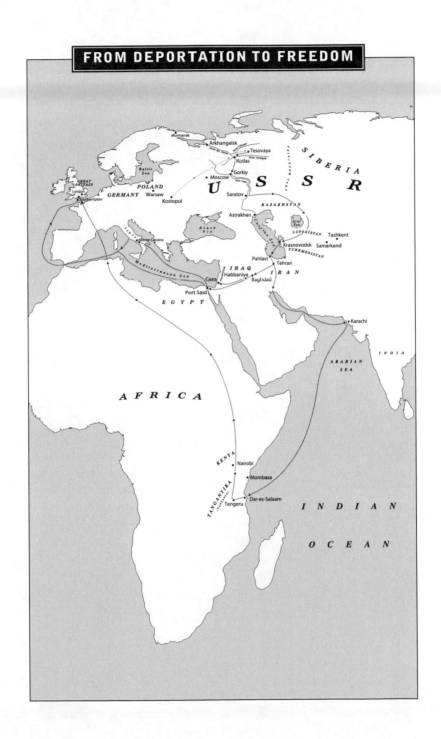

FROM DEPORTATION TO FREEDOM

Mumansk
Arkhangelsk
Tesovaya
Kotlas
Moscow
Gorkiy
USSR
SIBERIA
Baltic Sea
GREAT BRITAIN
London
Southampton
POLAND
GERMANY
Warsaw
Kostopol
Saratov
KAZAKHSTAN
Astrakhan
URAL MOUNTAINS
UZBEKISTAN
Tashkent
Aral Sea
Black Sea
Monte Cassino
Krasnovodsk
Samarkand
TURKMENISTAN
Pahlavi
Tehran
IRAQ
IRAN
Gaza
Habbaniya
Mediterranean Sea
Port Said
Baghdad
EGYPT
Karachi
INDIA
ARABIAN SEA
AFRICA
KENYA
Nairobi
Mombasa
TANGANYIKA
Tengeru
Dar-es-Salaam
INDIAN OCEAN

Contents

Helcia's Poems

MAPS AND SHADOWS

PRELUDE

Helcia

Angles of Memory *(Helcia)*

Everyone has a story.

Some stories are difficult to believe, though true. Others accurate, yet dull. Some difficult to tell—apart from the others. One story often spills into another, echoes, diverges before crossing trajectories again. The skeins once separated, can fray. To isolate the variable can unthread the most composed, even the most vain.

This is my story and my younger brother Henryk's story. My mother Zofia's and my father Andrzej's. My youngest brother Józef doesn't speak of these places. Somehow his memories were lost.

A story of war, shifting boundaries, alliances and ideologies. A story of mid-twentieth-century ice and burning sun.

History tells such stories, recorded through speech, shaded recollection. The human hand carves on stone, brushes ink to tablet, lines on a map, throws pottery on a wheel, carries a gun, pats the shoulder of another firmly *it will be okay*, coaxes the infant to sleep, looks over the shoulder—and up ahead.

These gestures to understand, represent, make the past manageable—to pass the book on. *Here is our chapter, remember us. Now what will you do—knowing all this?*

Spin the globe blindfolded and point to a country to see if it is still there. Take scissors and cut out the divisions between nations on a map. An exercise in rhetoric and chance.

Ancient themes reemerge: history repeating itself incorrigibly. Tenacious greed. The snake eating its own tail makes a circle, *alpha* and *omega*, a process, a spin.

> A free country is not free not to go to war.
> *War*, it is said, *the path to freedom.*

Yes, there are many stories and many ways to tell one story. Manifold shadows of one tree. Though the limbs can be truncated and leaves shorn.

Some need to speak, to tell the others; others cannot bear to remember, relive. They cannot be relieved, afford to recollect, risk a bankruptcy of the worst kind.

One can be born into a line of kings, another the son of a soldier. The daughter of the king could not marry the peasant's son. The peasant's son dreams of a marble, the eye of a saint on a stick for public display.

Some are born into a way of worshiping or not worshiping God. To be born on one side of a barbed wire fence or stone wall, identified with a group of people as better, or turned away—*you do not belong. You are not one of us. You cannot stay*—

If lucky, take your family and leave. If separated from your family, look through the debris. There are agencies to verify. Records of teeth. Fill out the forms properly. We will send a flag even if you cannot speak. Even if there is no longer a country.

There are those who worship power, money, prestige. The ego trying to press itself into the pages of history, unable to admit defeat. *I was here x years and this is what is left. Remember me.*

One's character, place, and time: the x, y, and z.
The fields, the skies, and angle of memory.

Some are born without proper shelter, without the luxury of food, safety, academic training, access to employment, *ladder mobility*. Others born into mansions, many born into disease. So many variables seemingly shaken in a hat— or perhaps pre-mapped, depending on one's beliefs. Who is to say?

This is my family's story. A story of starvation and betrayal. One chess game of many in the tome of history, yet a complicated game with repercussions nonetheless.

A story of survival for a few—a story of intense cold and heat. A story of mid-twentieth-century ice and burning sun.

A story of maps and shadows.

Displaced Persons

The cartographer, busy rearranging borders,
does not hear the gunshots, glimpse the people
lined up behind their possessions, aching
not to turn back, not to remember [home].

He hardly notices the country cut out
and hidden. Severed from history,
lost cities undo memory's veils.

The frozen bluebird wrapped in tree dust
will not survive. This, a fact, or arguably
an omen. *Take your family and leave*
salvage what to carry and what hour.

The wounds of hunger can deepen
bones' vacuous sockets eaten by time
that stills and fallows.

Not knowing the aftermath,
the proper names for infinite
waiting and disarray, the fear
of being useless.

Night, the circumference we stay inside
at the margins of quiet, begging strangers
for variations of kindness.

Counting up deaths, there were many.
Those ghosts that slip, sleeves pulled that
come undone. All this undid
what we knew, feeble specks
lost in the cosmos.

Henryk

CHAPTER 1

Our Orchards (*Henryk*)

Eastern Poland, 1939–1940

SOME DATES change the world irrevocably. What is done cannot be undone. No matter how well- or ill-conceived. One plane or two or ten piercing invisible lines, seeking enemy flesh.

A page of history that can never be torn out permanently. Things tend to catch up. Even when they are buried or ripped out. And it's impossible for people to go on the same, though many pretend while sweeping the ashes under the expensive silk carpet. It depends where the lines are drawn. Maps and agreements that may or may not be honored, upheld. Memory, selective. Paper and flesh can be burned.

The history books my sister, Helcia, loved—would become unreal, unwritten. The Helcia that was light, flipped her honey hair and skipped with her books about lost cities, golden ash. Before the stone pages made her heavy. The then-unwritten pages that would unfold us. One group of people fighting another; the variables, teams and players switching, faking the others out.

T he fading hours of twilight fell quickly that late summer of 1939. I was eleven and a half years old, and like the other boys of my *osada* (village), had that feeling of youthful invincibility burgeoning in every vein. There was an ominous sense that the village talk of another large-scale war could come to fruition, but we shook that thought off gallantly. We were too busy playing our own war games, striving to be like our fathers, who were all decorated war heroes before we were born.

The wind unsettled the pine trees and disheveled the girls' long hair. Asia, Kasia, Magdalena, Małgosia, Dorota, Helcia and her friends. My peers and I didn't know exactly when it happened, our new interest in how the light transformed the shades of their hair from molasses to amber to honey—and in the new, subtle curves of their bodies. We could hear them laughing in the distance, there in the intricate spaces of a neighbor's farm. Their hushed giggles intrigued us, but we remained awkward around them, afraid of appearing foolish, so we poised ourselves, hoping to get a distant glimpse, a keyhole into their world.

"Come in, synu (my son). Supper on the table," my father summoned from afar. He was more than likely still feeding our farm animals. I could barely hear the newborn sheep bleating to be fed; they were born a few days ago and still wet from birth. Our watchdog Hałas, named for his noisiness, barked also, fulfilling his job to keep foxes and other predators away from our horses, sheep, pigs and chickens. I had finished cleaning the barn about a half hour prior. Father and I tried to alternate between cleaning and feeding; his call to me signaled he was almost finished feeding all our livestock.

I knew that Mama, Helcia and Józef would be waiting in the kitchen to begin dinner. But like the other boys my age,

I pretended not to hear the voice of my father—and stayed out as long as possible, finding a rugged way through the dark of the orchards. We played dead to be hidden, to squeeze more hours of nightfall, intrigued as we were by the mystery of dark. And the darkness of our own games.

There was an urgency in being boys, sharing the space outdoors without elders, practicing to be men in front of witnesses, to convince ourselves in the process. We challenged our peers while smoking cigarettes like our fathers, climbing the gnarled trees, stepladders to the heavens. We longed for the girls to be proud of us as our mothers revered our fathers, hoping they looked curiously at us through their own windowpanes.

Aside from our awkwardness with the adolescent girls of our village, we were cocky, not believing the rumors of the impending assault on our country and our homes, the land our fathers were given in gratitude for their bravery in the Polish–Bolshevik War of 1919–1920, the war fought to retain Poland as an independent country after more than a hundred-year hiatus. From 1795 to 1918 Poland was essentially erased from maps, history books and globes, partitioned by Prussia on the west, Russia on the east, and Austria on the south. As a reward for reinstating Poland's eastern borders after the Polish–Bolshevik War, my father and forty other veterans of the Polish Army were each awarded a plot of thirty-plus acres to farm, land in southeastern Poland that previously had been part of Russia. The land wasn't considered very valuable, as it was grooved by ditches and foxholes remaining after the front lines had crisscrossed several times in the last phases of the war.

The newly formed Polish government had said *thank you for a job well done; try your hand at the sandy earth and see if you can thrive, if you are as skilled a farmer as a soldier.*

After enduring the trenches, our young fathers scoffed, tapping the burnt tobacco from their pipes, saying *thank you for the place for our sons to grow as tall as the pines, as fertile as the land we will cultivate with hard toil for our bravery's reward. The place where we will work, put away our rifles and war medals in chests of drawers, and live out the rest of our days with our wives and children, cultivating potatoes, barley, rye, oats, wheat. There is nothing else we need.*

They were young when the government gave them the land to farm in 1922—my father just twenty-two, the same age as my mother; both born at the turnstile of the twentieth century. Father had known my mother in Blizne from grammar school. He thought it would be prudent to marry while starting the farm, and therefore returned to his place of birth to ask Zofia to marry him. Orphaned since seventeen, she was living in her brother's house. My father's mother had died unexpectedly of pneumonia when she was almost fifty. Mama and Tata quickly became each other's family. After the hardship of the first several years, in which other settlers helped them build their house and farm buildings and vice versa, the following years proved abundant. They were tired but content on their own land in Piłsudczyzna, as the farm village was called. Little by little, the crops improved.

And then there would be the extension of their family—Helcia, the eldest child in 1925, myself three years later, and (after losing an infant son) Józef in 1935. We grew up with tools in our hands, scythes and trowels. Helcia's tools were mainly for cooking and sewing. I worked outside with my father even in the winter, for the farm entailed enormous labor.

We all rose early to tend to the animals and crops. My

family employed a few workers for the fields during harvest time and a full-time man who helped with a wide range of chores on the farm and in the stables. We called him *Wujek* (Uncle) though he was not; he always had something for one of us in his pocket—a piece of candy, a carved bluebird for Józef. Even though we were not "blood," we considered him family. Calling a man "uncle" made him so; it had something to do with the level of respect given, the naming as *family*, *rodzina*, a word I would think about obsessively over the next decade.

Our settlement did not have its own school. Helcia and I walked two miles each way to a nearby town until our village constructed its own school in 1936. We walked even during the frequent snowstorms that punctuated winter. Often we walked in snow up to our waists and when we arrived at school, stood in front of the fire until we were warm and dry enough to focus on our studies.

Prior to September 1, 1939, our lives were filled with school and the mundane tasks of our land, crops and livestock. September 1, 1939: the first pivotal date in my life's chronology. The day the Germans attacked Poland, and began what was recorded unanimously in history books all over the world as the first day of World War II. The war we had not let ourselves contemplate seriously, announced itself in the form of German tanks at the western boundaries of our homeland, etching the day into history books with indelible red ink.

At four o'clock in the morning, before daylight, German planes bombed Polish border towns, some reaching as far as Warsaw. *Blitzkrieg*, "lightning war," as it would later be termed. The small Polish Air Force presented no match for the enormous firepower of over fifteen hundred German aircraft. We expected England and France to honor the treaty they had signed, in what we believed to be good faith, to join our forces in retaliation against Hitler and his plan to annihilate all Poles and again efface Poland from the world stage. Fifty-three hours after the attack on Poland, the British government declared war on Germany. Six hours later, France followed suit. A formal declaration of war without any actual assistance with soldiers or armaments, however, did not help the Polish cause.

In addition to the war between the two armies, Hitler targeted the civilian population, including women and children. Low-flying German planes slaughtered young girls picking potatoes in the fields from close range. The rest of the world did not want to see the image of the young girls in the field, an image that would become an iconic photograph of children cold-bloodedly murdered during war. Our parents and neighbors held their breath, still believing that it was just a matter of time before other countries and their diplomats would step in to halt such barbaric killings.

We kept waiting, restlessly, in disbelief. We waited for England and France to do something, to send help, military assistance, arms. We waited as the German tanks rolled in and the bombs fell from the sky on Warsaw, the heart of our country whose arteries would be critically shorn. Not without a desperate fight. Not without enormous courage and bloodshed.

The war was close, in the capital, yet far away. My father, like the other Polish veterans in our area, learned about the war on the radio. At all hours of the night that September, the radio that Tata owned (one of the few in the entire village) droned in the background amidst loud crackling static as neighbors filtered in and out to hear the latest update followed by quiet, nervous speculation that the children (hiding silently around door frames) were not to hear.

Seventeen days after the German invasion from the west, Russia invaded Poland from the east, as clandestinely planned. One week prior to the onset of the German invasion, Russia and Germany had signed the Molotov–Ribbentrop Pact, named for their respective foreign ministers. This non-aggression pact between Germany and the USSR included a secret protocol that divided Poland between its two rapacious neighbors. The new border would eventually run along the Bug River: west of that line, the Germans would be in control and to the east, the Russians. Poland's fate seemed geographically sealed once again by the implications of this document, covert Soviet– German collusion. The secret protocols to this non-aggression treaty would also impact Finland, Estonia, Latvia, Lithuania and Romania by similarly dividing those lands into German and Soviet spheres of influence.

We endeavored to continue with our daily routine as best we could, cognizant that German tanks ravaged Warsaw. It was nearly impossible to concentrate on school or anything else aside from the War for the next few months. Before this dual invasion from the west and then the east in September 1939, my homeland was something a boy my age didn't think excessively about. What is a country to an almost twelve-year-old who had not yet worn a uniform?

Our schoolboy camaraderie conditioned us to be nonchalant about such things, to be tough. Yes, we knew from school and from our fathers that Poland did not exist as a country for over one hundred years, but we believed that to be the past, dormant—nothing to do with us now. Those books were dusty and belonged to our grandfathers whom we did not have the luxury of knowing.

We took school for granted, as do all children who have not had education taken away. In the past we had consistently asked our teachers for more challenging questions instead of mechanical tests. True or false—too easy for addressing what we were learning to be complexities, shades of gray; the multiple choice test too convenient. We wanted no answers to choose from—longing to invent a new wheel and sign our names for posterity.

About a week after the Russians invaded eastern Poland, the Ukrainians formed a militia to replace the Polish police. Our *osada* was an oasis surrounded by Ukrainian villages. Historically, animosity and friction between Poles and Ukrainians had always existed. Most recently, the Ukrainians believed it was unfair that we were given free property instead of them.

While the Russians occupied our land, the Ukrainians were the "big shots" and repeatedly threatened to slit our throats and burn our buildings. My family was always ready to hide in the forest. Our wagon hitched to a pair of our horses was discreetly packed with supplies in case, at a moment's notice, we had to flee. A few friendly Ukrainians, whom we knew prior to the German and Russian invasions, would warn us, "It would be safer not to stay at home tonight." At least three times we left our house and hid overnight in the forest about three miles from our farm. Józef was scared until we told him we were playing a very important game that required absolute silence and "not tears from such a big boy," Mama cajoled.

We continued to attend school—with different teachers and

classes, however. Russian became mandatory; religion banned. The Russians strongly encouraged us to join the Komsomol, a Communist youth league that glorified Communism and Stalin.

Christmas was bittersweet that year. We were grateful to be alive and together but afraid of the next progression in the historical chain of events. On Wigilia (Christmas Eve) when we broke *opłatek* (the Christmas wafer), we hardly spoke to each other, exchanging the wafer quietly while avoiding eye contact.

That winter comprised a silent winter of waiting; a winter of walking on eggshells, pretending everything would be okay. Normalcy would resume. The Communist regime would falter in Poland, we wanted to believe.

During the predawn hours of February 10, 1940, the second date inscribed permanently in my family's chronology, nine days before my twelfth birthday, our watchdog Hałas barked furiously until all of us awakened. Within minutes, heavy pounding reverberated at our door.

"What is it?" I asked my mother. I was half asleep and feared that something may have happened to one of our neighbors. Or that someone we knew. . . I shook the thought off as a sleep-induced worry, but my mother did not motion to reassure me or to answer. My father peered through the shutters of their bedroom window.

He informed us quietly that Russian soldiers surrounded the house.

Within minutes, the tall, brawny soldiers in olive uniforms occupied our home. Their rifles were the magnetic focal points for all of us. Józef looked quizzically at their guns, seeming to wonder where our rifles were for this new, foreign game. As the oldest son, I amassed as much courage in my facial expression as I could to show that I was not afraid in front of my mother, wanting to help the situation somehow. I tried to be strong for Helcia (though she was three years older) and my brother Józef, who was not yet five years old and unable to comprehend the full impact of the sudden presence of these men behind their rifles with fixed bayonets.

Tata, my father. The Russian soldiers tied him with rope to a leg of the heavy kitchen table and left him facing a corner of the kitchen so that he could not see us. I'm sure he worried desperately about what they would do to us. The soldiers read the deportation order, making it clear that legally we were enemies of Russia and as such, would have to be relocated to prevent any sabotage of their supply lines. The soldiers ordered my mother, sister, brother and me to sit on the floor while they ransacked our house looking for arms, pulled drawers from dressers, and removed all the mattresses from our beds.

When they finished their thorough search of our home, they instructed us to begin packing. We had forty-five minutes to gather what we could carry. They spoke firmly and factually telling my mother specifically to pack sensibly, things to take with us, warm clothes, "useful" items. She complied as commanded without looking directly at their eyes, without challenging their succinct orders. I watched her hands shake ever so slightly as she removed the *pierzyna* (down quilt) from her and Tata's bed (the bed that we all sought when we were sick, scared, or had nightmares) to pack our belongings in it.

My mother bundled practical things as directed—dried meats, barley, flour, matches, heavy clothes. She nervously instructed Helcia and me to bring her our warmest things and asked Helcia to do the same for Józef. She discouraged Helcia from including any books, but I saw my sister conceal her dictionary in a sweater. One of her teachers had given her this dictionary a few years prior as a reward for being the top student in her Polish history and literature classes. Her piercing look begged me not to mention the hidden book to our parents.

Within a half hour, the Russian soldiers lined us up outside the house. Tata was unbound and stood close to our mother. It was unusually cold that morning and still dark with a multitude of stars piercing night's dark indigo palette. I remember looking up and noticing how clear the night loomed. The crisp glints of light, ironic.

"What will happen to our animals?" Helcia asked me in a whisper. "Will they starve or be mercifully slaughtered?"

I looked away, unprepared to answer.

The Russian soldiers ordered us to stack our possessions on a sled waiting outside our house. The Ukrainian driver whipped the horses that trotted briskly toward the railroad station, approximately six miles away.

As our sled arrived at the train station, we could see the countless other deported families from our settlement and from surrounding villages designated to share our journey. We had not been aware that the forty other families of our village were similarly being "processed" at the same time and were headed with us toward the same unknown destination. Thousands of dislodged Polish civilians, more people in one place than I had ever witnessed, nervously waited at the train station.

It could have been so much worse, I learned from others in our village. My father was not tortured, my mother and siblings, for now, unscathed. In other homes soldiers killed parents in front of their children; the children pushed along by the soldiers' rough shoves, without them.

Hour after hour, night after night, I thanked God for my parents and prayed for the young children without any. I kept wondering why we were being kept alive. Like the other men and boys in our settlement, my father and I, able-bodied free labor for the Russian workforce, were to prove valuable. Perhaps they spared the women and children so that the prospective workers would be able to concentrate and survive with some support and reason to live. I wasn't sure, but prayed we would all survive and that we would not be separated.

Our verdant orchards were receding quickly—the greenness foreshadowing the greenness of death. The color that settles in to replace the color of flesh. But we were cocky then, bragging with adolescent-inflated bravado of the place where we would become tall soldiers and strong farmers, herding sheep and cattle, where *all would not be lost.*

"Come in, synu," my father called again more urgently.

"Yes, Tata, I will be in soon." *I will find my way out of the shadows and darkness. I will join you, Mama, Helcia and Józef at the table. I will leave bravely and remember the orchards, our farm, my boyhood, our lost home, the obsolete borders of Poland. I will not forget what others said did not happen. I will urge Helcia to carve out the bloodspill with her pen.*

Train to Siberia

The horses dead and rotting in the barn
elude the threshold of imagining.

*A*wake, degraded, we are all strange[rs]
to sunlight, sustenance, and plans.

A cloud of bone, field of bone crosses
infinite array of grays shaping shadows.

The boy on a tall man's shoulders
probes splintered boards of our cattle car—

mangled limbs left by the train tracks
at the periphery of remembrance and sorrow.

Turn the pages of the Book, A–Z, string words
to wrap blankets *some of us, at least, will survive.*

Old Russian women sweep snow from the tracks.
Lost, they don't come back

though there is nowhere to go—
endless days of cold, hunger, and snow.

Helcia

CHAPTER 2

The Cattle Train (*Helcia*)

En Route Northeast, 1940

THE HORSES were dead and rotting in the barn. Someone was hiding in the cellar. Planes bombed our house. Józef was trapped in the fields and coaxed away by a German soldier.

"Józef, no! Run through the forest quickly. We'll find you, I promise. Don't cry. Hold the bluebird in your pocket that Wujek Jan carved for you. Look ahead and run! Remember what Tata has told us—the address."

"Tata, Tata, why can't you move?" Could he hear me? Why didn't he answer? Why was he covering his face with his bent arms? "Tata, it's Helcia. Open your eyes."

Father hid his war medals in a fireproof metal box in Poland, proud enough to preserve them for perpetuity but unable to confront the shiny metal and stiff ribbons every day. That chapter was over, he had thought. Perhaps he protected them for a future he hadn't yet completely envisioned, for a time when he would choose to remember or want someone else to know.

War humbled him; he couldn't talk about what he had seen in the Bolshevik War. Tata with his hands tied behind his back forever, somehow.

"It is better to forget, Tinia (little one)," he would whisper even before our deportation, without the slightest flicker of bitterness or doubt. "Those history and Polish books you carry all those miles to school and from room to room, so heavy, as eyelids before sleep pulls them shut."

Back then our gaze would catch and hold; my clear blue eyes probing his gray-flecked eyes for the pigment that bound us.

"Yes Tata, I know."

I have been told to stick to the facts, to what is real instead of imagined, to what can be touched instead of what is felt. I believe the intention of this instruction was kindness.

So, I shall begin with the facts and try to use them as a steadying branch over the abysses of night, hunger and terror. Others should know.

The Russian soldiers packed us forcefully into the fifty empty cattle cars that were waiting for us at the train station. In total, as a result of three separate evacuation phases, 1.5 million Poles from the eastern portion of our country were deported like us, forced on command to leave our home and what could not be carried, or be killed.

The soldiers pushed approximately sixty of us into each cattle car, which had two wooden shelves on each side, ten people to a shelf. Their guns nudged us; they were especially rough with the men. *You think you're tough, you think you're a soldier? You have no uniform now.*

There was a subtle undercurrent of insecurity, however; perhaps they realized that it was in some way arbitrary, that they were wearing the uniforms and not Tata and the other Polish veterans. On another day, the tides could turn—a queen removed quickly from the game of chess with one bullet, with one official document signed, one mass grave that would be vehemently denied. But I shall adhere to the facts for now.

There was a small, wood-burning stove in the middle of our cattle car, but no toilet facilities. One man cut a round hole in the floor with a hatchet he had brought from his farm. Someone else draped a blanket around the opening and that became our latrine for the unknown number of days ahead of us. We had no idea how long our journey would last, if we would see "normal" days again. I dreaded using this mock-toilet, but then the pain attacked and doubled me over, forcing me to confront the smell, the unsanitary conditions, and the degrading feeling of being reduced to an animal—while trying to stay balanced and not vomit the minimal contents in my stomach, as the dirty, portable barn jerked on the tracks.

We were incredibly hungry and found it difficult not to think of food, not to imagine what we would be eating at each meal, if we were home. I could smell fresh meat cooking in my memories and struggled not to salivate and not to cry. Aside from the cold scraps of fish or barley soup and slice of dark, waterlogged bread that we received every two or three days from the Russian soldiers, we subsisted on the food we brought from home—kasha, various grains, dried meats. We didn't know how long the food supply from our farm would last. It seemed strange that they were feeding us periodically, keeping us alive. I kept thinking we were being saved to be tortured or to be worked to our bones (a psychological and physical ossification), behind the scenes of war, implicated unwillingly. But at least we were alive, unlike other village family members. Many fathers of children my age and younger had mysteriously disappeared, those who were still active in the military and of significant rank. The Russians claimed that they must have fled, but there were no traces of any such conjectured journeys.

Hour after hour, unrelenting day after day, the clunking of the steel tracks droned, clacked, and droned. We were not informed of our destination but we could guess, given the order to pack warm clothes. Siberia, the northern place of historical exile depicted in nineteenth-century oil paintings that I had read about in school. The place of political eviction for fugitives, dangerous individuals and so-called "undesirables." Or in our case, an inconveniently located group of people with strong military affiliations. And I was the oldest, the ancillary mother of Henryk and Józef—in case anything happened to Mama—in case we were separated from the adults. In case we were lost.

The train stopped every forty-eight hours or so, usually to

pick up more coal for the two locomotives that were pulling and pushing the storage cargo of three thousand Poles. Immediately, as the train halted, a throng of restless gray bodies pressed against the door of the cattle car to jump off as soon as possible, to relieve hunger and claustrophobia. Eyes squinted against the sudden sun and the magnitude of the landscape, adjusted and immediately scanned the area for food, hoping for maybe some dried meat or mushrooms, or the vestiges of fish to make soup, speculating whether anything could be traded. The area was also hastily surveyed for a private place to urinate or defecate instead of the semi-public toilet on the train.

The Russian peasant women tasked with sweeping snow from the train tracks met our gazes nervously. They were being watched carefully by Russian soldiers. I noticed their shoes were in poor condition and they were missing teeth. They resembled the grandmothers of some of my schoolmates, a kerchief wrapped over their heads and tied at the chin.

The train was safer than being found as an escaped Russian prisoner. At least we were together.

Once back on the cattle cars, the monotonous rhythm of the train lulled me into fatigue and disturbing dreams. Images of the low-flying German war planes haunted me. I would see and hear them. Their drilling buzz chipped away at the ear bone and left an aftertaste of rusted metal. My stomach continuously sinking, a stone in an endless well, and I would wake up screaming, I thought. But my hysterical pleading for events to stop, for the planes, tanks and soldiers to move backwards, was muted somehow like the cries of many of the others, their faces twisted, surprised that there was no sound.

A stranger from another village shook me awake by the collar of my dress. *Ta dum, ta dum, ta dum,* the droning of the train hitting the tracks reminded me where I was. Nightmare, reorientation, sleep—the pattern kept repeating. Like the undulations of powerful storm waves, the rhythm of the train ultimately pulled me back under consciousness again. Some of the adults said I was fortunate for the reprieve, for the passing of empty time. Others knew that consistent lucidity would preempt my nightmares and looked at me with pity as I struggled to stay awake, not fall back into the clenches of threatening dreams. My eyes kept falling heavily, craving more escape, even if temporary. Drunk with sleep, images persevered, *the newborn sheep frozen, clouds of pink blood, a field of bone crosses.*

What day was it? Did it even matter? I drew a stick for each day on the inside back cover of my heavy dictionary. How many days were we on the train already? How many months since the War began? History, my favorite subject, along with literature and poetry—became esoteric subjects that betrayed us.

In between subsequent bouts of sleep, almost unconsciously, I remembered that the first poem known to be composed in the Polish language from the tenth or thirteenth century, "Bogurodzica," was a battle hymn sung by soldiers that begged "She who Gave Birth to God," for divine help, "win over for us, send to us." The Polish knights sang this anthem before the Battle of Grunwald in 1410, led by King Władysław Jagiełło against the Teutonic knights, and again during the battle with the Turkish army at Varna in 1444.

Few books, however, would record our particular journey and plight. Our story wasn't really relevant to the main story:

a battle of genocide. That story told in its own right and sadly, even challenged. The Poles often portrayed as involved because atrocities happened on our land. From the beginning of the Kingdom of Poland in the eleventh century, Poland was considered one of the most tolerant countries in Europe, and consequently attracted a large Jewish population. The Constitution of Poland adopted on May 3, 1791, the first modern, codified constitution of Europe, introduced political egalitarianism within its constitutional monarchy.

After Poland's nationhood had been stolen for over a century, its reestablished borders in the twentieth century again welcomed anyone who would work hard and reside within; religion a private matter. Why should one wear beliefs on the sleeve, a label for teams when there was already so much blood on our soil, war after war, to prove our right to sovereignty?

I couldn't help but contemplate how many lives would be lost, and for what end? Perhaps the thirst for blood innate, not thought out, the hunger for power, resources and control. That impulse to revise maps and ideology perpetually to be chiseled eventually into a monolithic statue, immortal in the pages of history. Assert power; seize land. The subtle intricacies of cause, effect and cessation. Claiming that one's God or lack thereof allows one group dominion over another, the birthright to greed. And so the history of the world had gone, one conquest after another. For gold, for passageway, for rights to basic necessities and the wealth there, the often taken-for-granted ability to move freely.

These were the things I contemplated on the train while struggling to stay awake, away from nightmares and even crueler dreams, monotonous hour after hour, day after day without sun. There were no windows save for small grated openings at each end of the cattle car. Occasionally a child would plead and venture up to the top ledge from the shoulders of a tall adult, attempting to peer through a crack between boards near the ceiling. The reflected flecks of daylight in the small child's eyes were amplified by those looking on, especially the few elderly among us who could barely stand while the train jolted ahead.

Idle chitchat with other teenagers on the train briefly passed some time. *I wonder what happened to so and so, do you remember that day in the orchards, that walk from school, that trick that was played on* . . .

We tried to keep the topics light in front of the adults, to half laugh whenever possible, before a weariness from talk, fumbling with what could be said, and sitting silent like Mama and Tata and the others their age and older. They would speak infrequently; the abrupt staccato notes of their unused voices off-key. Not the melodious voices left behind, tucked into the crevices of our childhood—the former version of my mother who sang in the kitchen, my father who chuckled as he tapped his pipe, thinking of his father perhaps. Mama's parents had both died years ago as well as Tata's mother. I couldn't fathom Henryk, Józef and me without Mama and Tata.

A to Z, "Andrzej" and "Zofia." They were everything to us— a portable family, a sacred relic of home. A to Z. I practiced exercises in language, like scales of a piano, variables from which to construct a jerry-rigged machine of hope to get my darkest thoughts off the ground, emerge from the underworld. I attempted to arrange credible sentences imbued with the belief that *some of us, at least, would survive.* I thought of all the possible scenarios—the various ways to arrange the future, the days, hours, the dread . . . Until the train pulled me back under consciousness, folded me back into sleep momentarily where I struggled with images and dreams, *the horses were dead and rotting in the barn.*

I ripped out blank space from the margins of my dictionary and wrote out words sometimes while the train was lurching. Once free under the sky while the train stopped, I'd hide the little pieces of paper with my slanted print so as to forget what the papers said, impart them to someone else. I thought of the Wailing Wall in a faraway land and understood the impulse to offer up the prayers, to be relieved of them—and how in Japan, prayers were etched on thin pieces of wood and then burned. Prayers too heavy for anyone but a God—or a reminder that all material things are fleeting.

Some passages of time were elastic and stretched for eternities, stitched with questions. *Would we survive? Would we be tortured?* Our stomachs consistently empty.

Our home, our farm, our property, our livestock and beautiful orchards retreating from my memory. My eyes viscous with tears that welled but that I would not shed now, nor in those final glances behind us as we trudged toward the unknown, fearing that my younger brothers, Henryk and Józef, would see and remember me, the way I remembered Tata.

I could not banish the tenacious reappearance of the photo my recollection had crystallized—even though I did not want to remember: Tata with his hands tied behind his back to our kitchen table, the place where we gathered as a family. I wanted that image obscured like the stifled shrieks from my nightmares, blurred—but it was sharp and clear, and would not be drowned, obliterated. Henryk sitting next to me on the stone floor quickly hiding all traces of fear as if nonchalantly swallowing a sharp object. Four-year-old Joseph confused.

Were we playing a new game and if so, why were we all deathly afraid and where were our guns? His eyes darted quickly from Mama to soldier, to me to soldier to Tata, to Henryk and back again.

Who would feed our hens, sheep and other animals? With no one to take the eggs, there would be many mouths to feed. Would they freeze in the barn or die of hunger, or were they already slaughtered? I longed to ask Henryk again; maybe he would know after thinking further about this question. He was not as preoccupied as Tata nor would he say the question was frivolous, as Mama would scowl. She had aged in those moments the Russian soldiers appeared at our door, fear draining from her face instantly so we, her children, could remember her as strong. But there had been a cost; her soft skin pulled taut to hide expression, to tighten the drum of silence.

Perhaps it was the rare dream that dragged me back into sleep and the series of nightmares. I was on the farm practicing the words to a song I was composing while collecting eggs from the chickens. I was happy. The boy I liked, Tomek, liked me. Joasia had told me that day on the long walk from school. The twilight sun illuminated me. I was warm, pleased.

Mama was stroking my hair while I moved in and out of sleep. For a split second I thought I was resting in Mama and Tata's bed on our farm in Poland. I heard the rooster's cry pierce morning and the sheep bleating.

The disparity upon waking stabbed sharply. The contrast of the grimy, foul-smelling cattle train against a lovely remembrance or vision:

> We packed and fled before the Russian soldiers arrived. We hid in the forest again. The night was quiet and calm, the open air refreshing. The

31

evening breeze circulated the pleasant redolence
of roses and honeysuckle. We would be home soon,
when daylight crept up through night—

Try to stay awake Helcia, Henryk pleaded. When I finally
refocused the image of him sitting next to me, I realized he
had transformed. From the boy of jokes and games and secret
cigarettes to a young man still trying not to show his new,
adult fear.

On the eighteenth day of our journey (according to my tally
of days), when the train stopped, the desperate stampede broke
an old man's leg and the Russian commander demanded that he
be left behind. Mama told me not to look, not to remember such
things. So I tried to think of other memories, all the things I
missed, the smell of clean clothes and meat cooking, the summer orchards, our animals, the sky. The animals that would be
waiting to be touched and fed while Henryk completed his
chores quickly to join the other boys of our village, our
unreachable home.

I longed for the orderly rows of desks at school, books, paper
to write on with precise pencils, the poise and confidence of
our teachers, my friends, the boy I had grown fond of, Tomek. I
prayed that he and his family survived.

I missed being preoccupied with mathematical problems,
ancient history, mythical themes to study and imagine, to pon-
der during the two-mile walk home from school to our farm,
thinking the whole way freely under the expanse of sky, letting
the pieces of the day flicker and settle. The focus on learning
suddenly extricated along with the ramifications—boredom
and the sense of falling behind, left out of history. Would our

minds slow down and others move ahead, permanently take control?

On several of the torn papers I had written the mantra Henryk and I rehearsed even at the cusp of waking and sleep: *44 Barber Street, Windsor, Conn.* We feared our memory would be corroded by our continuous hunger. We repeated this phrase to Józef in case he could remember, if necessary. *44 Barber Street, Windsor, Conn.*, the address my father urged us to memorize and to recite if any of us ever escaped Russia alive. Even if alone, *we must not hesitate* but *plead for assistance* to reach *44 Barber Street, Windsor, Conn. In far-off America. Our uncle lives there and will take us into his home.*

This address became a rectangular flag of hope we waved to the rhythm of the train, staked out in the fields of our imaginations, where Wujek Janek, who emigrated from Poland in 1912, would answer. *Yes, you are my family, stay. I will feed you, offer light and heat. I will send for the others, if still alive. If not alive, proper burials. We will sit at the table together. You will have new roots stronger than the trees in your lost orchards. And never starve again.*

After twenty-eight days, twenty-eight sticks drawn on the inside back cover of my dictionary, we finally arrived at our destination at the end of the railroad line, the town of Kotlas at the junction of the Severnaya Dvina and Vychegda Rivers, three hundred miles from the port of Arkhangelsk and the White Sea in the northern part of European Siberia.

Russian soldiers unloaded us carelessly from the train and haphazardly stacked our possessions on sleds that we were instructed to walk behind through the vast Siberian forest.

The claustrophobia of the cattle car, the heat and smell from the number of us in one unsanitary, small space was replaced, superimposed, with a vastness of desolate, open, cold landscape. The temperature initially hovered around zero degrees Fahrenheit, considered moderate for the region, but very quickly the winds intensified and the temperature plummeted. I was both dazed and frightened by the expanse of frozen earth and ominous, dark sky. How easy it would be to stumble, fall down and be left behind, layered over by new snow and ice, the windchill biting at flesh.

We stopped overnight at school gymnasiums in small towns or villages and tried to sleep before resuming our journey the next morning. We were all so awkward with one another, too nervous for banal chitchat. There seemed to be no sound, just an endless progression of gray photographs moving lugubriously.

On the third day walking behind the sled, finally we arrived at our destination. It was a logging camp built by those who were deported twelve years prior from the eastern part of Poland that Russia had appropriated. There were several log cabins in the middle of a forest of thirty- to forty-foot-tall spruces, hemlocks and sporadic birches.

White. Pure cold. Fifty below windchill. Cold white frozen snow. A coldness in the bones that cannot be shaken. A blank white landscape, empty like the slate of consciousness waking up. Waking in the cold. Woken by hunger, concentrating to forget its power and inducement of stupor.

What is there really to say about the cold? A void backdrop for thoughts until too tired, a blanket of nothingness, too cold and too hungry to sleep.

The landscape, a strange, unreal white canvas of snow, wind and ice: walks to the makeshift village, the other barracks, a wagon ride, watching the men leave before daybreak to trudge for over an hour to work in the forest... felling enormous trees, rushing home, thinking their cold thoughts... pulling the unsteady benches from the table...

What is there to remember but the cold? Childhood nonetheless, stolen as so many childhoods. The cold as bitter as the tobacco in Tata's pipe, vodka thrown back in the throat before and after a paltry meal (or at the time the meal should have been) to chase away the cold. The cold tearing at our faces, fingers, toes. No, there is no accurate way to describe the cold.

These are the facts, plus images, thoughts... and fear. Henryk said I must remember and record the events along with the magnitude of their hunger and shadows.

Ice Garden

Euclid's frozen geometric planes,
layer upon layer. Ice etching thin tree limbs,
glittery before snapped down.

Opalescent pillows glint too few sun-hours
to lie down in the cold wing-bones that rib
the sky. This scrim of the inner room

the door of some other *now*, the book
of *will* unknown. The book of *how*
and *why* drowned, encrusted under.

Sisyphus longed for a beginning, middle,
and end to make it all bearable or seem
to have a context. The shortest distance

between two points can be viole[n]t
those wounds in the armpits
wary at the lookout, ready to bow

and disregard history's narrative.
Too many deeds untold, buried perfunctorily
eyes twitching in the sharp cold

moving, scanning the taiga for tomorrow's
small death, frozen rabbit, another absence
to carry in the book unlocked.

The ice calls, breaks, and echoes,
slips focus. The ear aches begging
to quell windchill to dream

emerald orchards where *all*
will not be lost. Hungry, but alive.
The workers stay busy

naming components, counting steps,
counting trees, in a series, measuring
the cage of betrayal. Not to slip

the old man's hoarfrost trench coat
his memories of food and sun, a glorious death.
I have gone and the delay, the wind-throb
is over, what was lost.

[I have told you].

Andrzej

CHAPTER 3

Frozen Planes (*Andrzej*)

Siberia, 1940–1941

MY DAUGHTER says there is nothing to say about the cold, how to accurately describe those eternal days of Arctic wind and ice. The endless darkness and temperature as low as fifty to sixty degrees below zero.

Helcia's latest fallen scrap of paper described:

>*Euclid's frozen geometric planes*
>*ice heavy on tree limbs pulling*
>*thin branches down.*

My oldest. Would she continue shedding these tiny papers folded into the smallest parcels throughout her life, or were they skins of war? I shook my head, smoking a cigarette while staring up at the forty-foot hemlock and spruce trees. Smoking seemed to keep us warmer, gave us something else to focus on, and subtly tempered thinking.

I often hear her at night. Helcia, the one who pulls words down from the ether to describe what others cannot or dare not recount:

>*the muted blur of bruised winter suns,*
>*piercing animal cries, those lost sleeping.*

She has grown up too quickly after being sent from her girl-hood into the intense days on the train, hungry, muttering in her sleep, her chattering teeth clenched repeatedly against the cold or cruelty of her imaginings.

Helcia, who laments there is no way to step outside the cold and see it from afar, continues writing phrases on torn papers that she hides in the seams of her tattered clothes or tucks into her dictionary:

> *mangled limbs left by the train tracks,*
> *skeletons in the forest stark against hemlocks*
> *and frozen snow pillows.*

> *We are all so tired; the pillows burn*
> *our memories of food*
> *and sun.*

All able-bodied men and boys roughly between twelve and fifteen, like Henryk, were mandated to work in the Siberian taiga felling trees. We left the barracks at six o'clock in the morning, walked for an hour through five to six feet of snow, worked for eight to ten hours, and then walked nearly three miles to return, arriving back at our barracks between six and eight in the evening. We left and returned in the Arctic dark, but it was the cold that was more difficult to withstand.

The windchill pierced our bones as we trudged over frozen layer upon layer of snow and ice several miles to the forest and back again. One step, two steps; three steps, four steps; five steps, six steps; seven steps, eight steps; nine steps, ten steps; eleven. . . (left, right; left right; left right; left right. . .) When I reached a hundred, I started my silent counting all over again. The numbers offered something abstract to focus on and the counting prevented my pace from slackening and gave the illusion of progression (mathematical and geographical, at least). Henryk followed a few paces behind me.

A group of several work brigades left the barracks at the same time and returned together also. We were each assigned to a brigade. No one was late; a brigade could be penalized for not meeting a quota or "norm." The men of the barracks comprised six brigades, each consisting of eight men and two to three boys.

The boys Henryk's age were responsible for shoveling a radius of six feet of snow that was eight feet deep from around each tree, so that the older men could cut the tree not higher than one foot from the ground with a two-man saw. At the end of the day all saws and axes were turned over to the Russian camp *piłostaw* who would sharpen them, so they would be ready for use the next morning. The routine was a bit comforting in some ways; in other ways, incredibly monotonous.

The massive hemlock, birch or spruce teetered toward its fast, gravitational decline—a violent thunder crackled as the tree crashed in slow motion through the snow and ice. At first the sound and sight were breathtaking. Everyone evacuated the immediate area quickly and then stopped to watch in astonishment. Very soon, however, the thunder and crashing became an ordinary signal of the day, an inconvenient distraction for reaching one's norm, though one still had to move immediately out of the way, which had become second nature almost instantly.

Non-workers lined up at three o'clock in the morning to ensure that the rations did not run out; each non-worker was entitled to two hundred grams of waterlogged bread. The workers were given their ration of five hundred grams in the forest. No one could afford not to work, as hungry as we all were. "Those who do not work, do not eat," the Soviet dictate droned in our frozen ears.

Each log, depending on its thickness, had to be cut a certain length. There were norms established for each man and brigade. Not meeting a norm would result in a cut in food ration; exceeding a norm would merit a small bonus of a few rubles. At the end of the day the *lesomajster* (superintendent of the logging operations) stamped the ends of the logs and recorded which brigade should receive credit.

The output of cut lumber, the number of cubic meters of logs cut, was attributed to the appropriate brigade. The Russian management encouraged the brigades to compete with one another over which could cut the most timber. The competition propelled the workday to go by faster and kept us productive, but we knew who the real winners were, no matter which brigade placed first.

After we observed how the *leśomajster* stamped each individual log, we learned the trick of increasing our production norms substantially. We would cut a log a few inches longer than the minimum measurement and after the *leśomajster* stamped the end of a specific log and recorded it in his book, we would cut off the last few inches of the stamped log, dispose of the removed "excess" end in the ongoing fire, move its location and have the same log stamped for a second time, thereby increasing our production significantly. We couldn't pull off this trick with every piece of lumber, and understood it was the most profitable to do so on the thickest ones. The thicker the log, the easier to make one's quota.

Every ten or fifteen minutes, we pinched our cheeks and nose to determine if we could still feel them. If not, I instructed Henryk, he should grab a handful of snow and vigorously rub the exposed areas of the face to restart the circulation of blood. If one of us spit, a piece of ice formed before reaching the ground.

The boys cut the smaller branches to heap onto the fire, ensuring that the flames weren't extinguished until it was time to return to our camp. When too cold to hold the axe or the timber, we put our hands in front of the fire for several minutes. There wasn't much time to waste, however, to fulfill the daily quota to receive the ration of bread and soup.

At around noon each day, which never arrived soon enough because we were desperately hungry and practically frostbitten, a horse and sleigh arrived from the camp. The small kitchen staff from our settlement brought a large kettle of boiling soup, usually split pea or onion, and our rations of bread.

There was nothing extra to spare as the portions of soup were measured precisely. The boys Henryk's age received only two hundred grams for their bread ration even though it was mandatory that they assist the working men.

The hot soup warmed us and made it possible to work for the rest of the day. We ate slowly enough to savor each hot swallow without the soup getting cold—a delicate balance that we soon mastered.

The thick trees we were severing were used mostly for railroad ties, the medium-sized ones to build additional barracks, and the thinnest trees for export to England, mainly for building bridges over rivers for expedition of military operations. The lines of commerce ironic: Russia was selling timber to an enemy at that time, but there were few other resources to financially support the Soviet war effort. The men not assigned to fell trees like us had been tasked with building log cabins for future forced laborers.

Before our arrival, there were already barracks built by the Ukrainians and Byelorussians who were deported in the 1930s as part of Stalin's "systematic removal" of all Polish people in the Ukraine and Byelorussia. Those exiled before us would be invaluable for tips on how to survive. Stalin's methodical purging of the Byelorussians that culminated in 1936 comprised the first deportation of an entire ethnic group by the Soviet Union. Czarist Russia had utilized Siberia for exiles since the seventeenth century. When the Bolsheviks gained power in 1917, they continued to employ Siberia for relocating those deemed "undesirables."

In addition to the Poles who were deported with us in February 1940 in the first wave, there were two waves in April and June of 1940. After the arrival of each group, the local officials assigned deportees to individual barracks. Each barrack consisted of four or six rooms, each room with a large stove in the middle. In our room there were three families; fourteen people in all. The men constructed three separate beds out of wood, one for each family. The beds had removable boards and were opened only at night. During the day, the boards were folded and stacked along the wall to serve as benches.

Our shelter looked like military camp quarters and served mainly to harbor fire and keep the harsh windchill and ever-accumulating snow at bay. The majority of log cabins consisted of large rooms, usually three families occupying one room, as in our case. Most families consisted of two adults and two or three children. Our living quarters were tight, but at least we weren't as crammed as in the cattle cars. The children didn't mind sleeping on shelves. The men took turns keeping the fire going throughout most of the night. If it wasn't danger-ously cold, the fire could be banked with ashes for several hours allowing everyone to sleep or at least lie down.

The first thing each morning at around four thirty, one man from each room had to go to the nearby forest, find a dead tree, cut it down, and then split it into sections light enough to carry to the barracks. The pieces were further cut into logs about twenty-eight inches and split, if necessary. The water for cooking and washing had to be carried from the nearby river in two buckets hooked onto a piece of bent wood shaped to fit the carrier's shoulders. The first person who ventured to the river brought an axe to chop a hole in the ice that had refrozen overnight. It was amazing how quickly we morphed into the routine that the harsh landscape and our captors demanded.

The fire in the large stove served for both cooking and heating. In each barrack there were two rustic toilets, no toilet paper and no running water. For a couple of rubles people subscribed to a local paper, which was needed to roll cigarettes from loose tobacco and to wipe after relieving oneself. No one actually read the Russian paper; some knew a bit of Russian to speak and understand verbally from living near Ukrainians and from the children's mandatory Russian classes after the Soviet occupation of Poland in 1939. Very few could read the Russian Cyrillic alphabet, entirely different from the Polish alphabet, but the paper was valuable as kindling and toilet paper.

I was proud of Zofia, Helcia and Henryk for not complaining; instead, they trudged forward in their minds and wills very courageously. Józef did not understand what was going on and soon stopped asking, "When are we going home, Tata? Why can't we eat? Where are you going? Can I come with you?" We worried about his lack of nutrients the most, fearing he would stop growing.

When an occasional package arrived at camp from a deportee's family back in Poland, we prayed for some powdered milk that someone would trade with us for Józef, or some dried meat. It was strange to have an address in the middle of the Siberian forest:

> Settlement: Tesovaya
> Post Office: Kharitonov
> District: Solvychegodsk
> Region: Arkhangelsk

We knew none of the packages would be addressed to us; we had very little family left in Poland. If they were still alive and still in Poland, we were sure they would have nothing to spare.

Occasionally, a package arrived for someone deceased whose next of kin hadn't been notified. The Russian officials quickly confiscated those parcels. We thought of writing to the senders but their return addresses were snatched away—and even if we could write back, the words had to be chosen very carefully as all correspondence was censored. *Dear Pan and Pani* (Sir and Madam), *your grown children have been killed arbitrarily by causes unknown. We will bury them properly in the spring. We're doing all we can for your grandchildren. Send some bread, flour, dried milk, or meat. Who knows how long we will survive.*

After six long months of enduring the dire conditions of Siberia, to our disbelief, we received a package addressed to us. My brother Staszek sent us a large piece of leather that was worth more than a piece of gold when trading in the neighboring villages. The letter inside expressed Staszek's worry that the leather would not reach us, explaining that he had to at least try to send us something that would be valuable. There were other sentences that had been covered with dark ink, clearly censored by Russian officials, that we each tried to read, imagining what a sentence that length of Staszek's handwriting could possibly convey. The only thing agreed upon as a family was that we should save the precious leather for an emergency.

It was impossible to forget about home. To relinquish those acres, memories and plans. The Russian soldiers with their guns and orders on our land and the train ride haunted night and even acute moments of day without warning, pulling one off guard back to the tracks, the invisible vanishing point, the present without a known destination. Starving poor by the road left hugging the periphery of tree shadow or track, as one of Helcia's papers claimed. It was said that these forced labor camps weren't meant to keep us alive—the hard, physical work and the paltry rations of food were not equally matched, designed to slowly kill us after getting as much work from us as possible. There was no way to escape and if we did, there was nowhere to go. We would merely be beckoning death to arrive more quickly.

Two people in our camp had died already from pneumonia. They couldn't be buried until spring when the ground thawed. I was afraid of dying in the taiga, leaving my children and Zofia. Afraid of failing them as their father, as a husband and as a man. These thoughts visited me during the nights mainly. The coldest nights on the planet. We slept with all our clothes on. We had no soap or means to wash ourselves. As a result of poor hygiene, the clothes we wore and subsequently all the barracks were infested with bugs. The first insects were bed-bugs, then cockroaches that flew across the room as soon as we turned down the kerosene lantern. At times these bugs were more of a nuisance than the cold itself.

It was difficult to sleep in such circumstances, compounded by a terrible hunger that deepened every day. Wolves could be heard at night howling with their own hunger. We told Józef that they were dogs like Hałas back at our farm.

Helcia woke up one sleepless night sobbing hysterically, whispering to Zofia amidst gasps, that she couldn't see any-thing, that she was blind. She wept softly throughout that entire night.

Her vision returned with daylight, but she could not see at night for more than two weeks. We learned from some of the villagers that her condition, "night blindness," resulted from not having enough vitamins. One of the women instructed Zofia to feed Helcia the liver from a calf to restore essential nutrients. It took several days for Zofia to find a calf that a villager would trade. It cost us the large piece of leather from Poland and a variety of other items assembled and scrutinized before the deal was secured. It was impossible to mask our desperation. Within a few days of eating the calf's liver, Helcia could see at night again. Our prayers were answered. Poor Helcia. How I missed seeing her on the farm so happy. My oldest, my only girl. A smaller, slightly different version of her mother.

The windchill through our bones. The letters of the alphabet, beginning and end of the cold—A to Z—Helcia muttering in her half-sleep. *These are my bookends,* the paper once unrolled, claimed. Zofia and I unable to understand the broken poetry that occasionally slipped from Helcia's dress or dictionary, her attempts to solidify the sequence of events. Of course, Helcia had smuggled a book to bring with her, not the Bible as Zofia would have chosen but a dictionary, *the encyclopedia of language, of man,* she eloquently justified when Zofia discovered her hidden book. She carefully guarded the book knowing that the paper was valuable.

Helcia had grown so thin, like Henryk and Józef. And their mother, no longer the Zofia of the orchards, her long amber hair unruly in the night wind, the girl I had known in Blizne in grammar school. She looked much older and more serious than the young woman I had found when I went back to my town of birth and childhood to ask for her hand in marriage, to help me create a home on the farm, to build a family as newlyweds. She no longer accompanied her hard work with Polish ballads, no longer gazed through the small kitchen window to admire the land, the crops, the then-thriving children who were now quite literally a shell of what they had been, their lives prior to our forced exile.

If the temperature dropped colder than forty degrees below zero, the *lesomajster* notified one of the brigadiers that there would be no work that day, for it was impossible to survive. On those days we took turns tending to the essential fire in the barracks and mostly slept to forget the hunger, since we would not receive our pea soup and slice of bread that day. We slept to pass time, to rest from the hard labor, to forget. But the gnawing hunger and infestation of insects made it difficult to fall asleep and impossible to forget where we were.

The children old enough to be out of danger (unlike the youngest such as Józef who could not survive outside) sledded across the taiga ice, over hills and through trees on planks of wood, grateful for such days without school, not perceiving the ramifications of the too few hours of light. The men my age and older envied their boyhood. I think even Henryk did. He understood more than I anticipated; the War had expedited his manhood.

Freezing day after day, month after month of only three to four hours of sun in the Siberian taiga that stretched from the Ural Mountains to the Pacific Ocean. The only two holidays we were given off aside from the days too dangerously cold to survive, were May 1st and the day of the October Revolution. We worked Christmas and Easter, Saturdays and often on Sundays. At least in the summer there would be berries to pick and mushrooms, the earlier exiles told us—to instill some hope for alleviating our intensifying hunger and despair. Conversely, we were also told, there would be mosquitoes and small flies that would infiltrate any protective netting. Insects that would try to feed off us, no matter how severely malnourished we would be by then.

This scenario was difficult to imagine as heavy sheets of snow fell rapidly, spiraling in our faces with the aggressive winds. The Arctic blizzard had started an hour prior to the end of our workday and the walk back was taking hours due to the poor visibility and pull of winds.

Eighty-seven steps, eighty-eight steps; eighty-nine steps, ninety steps; ninety-one steps, ninety-two steps; ninety-three . . . Almost back to camp . . . I could see in the far distance Zofia with Helcia and Józef peering through the door of the small log cabin we shared with three other families. She resembled the Black Madonna of Częstochowa, the sacred protector of Poland, Hodegetria, She Who Shows the Way, with her young child and with a village girl perhaps. Her face darkened by enemy fire and scarred by Hussite swords. I was almost there—not *w domu* (at home), that word removed by the Russian orders—was almost back with them after walking nearly two hours during the blizzard through the frozen forest with Henryk after yet another interminable day in the cold.

They were framed in the doorway, waiting for us peacefully it seemed and for a moment, they appeared as gray diaphanous ghosts, their faces wizened, their limbs attenuated. I thought I saw my parents behind them and clenched my eyes shut. They had been dead for many years. I recognized my mother's cornflower blue eyes and my father's strong jaw—

Had I fallen in the snow, knocked out cold and was now dreaming? A vision before death of my wife, daughter and youngest son, shadows of their former selves in Poland, their faces drained of color.

No, I shook my head and looked back at Henryk. I was awake and pushing tiredly through the snow in heavy cracked boots that had been tied and taped and re-taped. *Ninety-four steps, ninety-five steps; ninety-six* . . . Yes, we were cold but there would be something hot to drink even if just hot water and a fire inside. At least we were together.

Dark day after day walking, counting, shivering, working, smoking, walking, counting, worrying, praying for the harsh winter to end, for the days to include more light, warmth, vegetation—more food. Long night after night, month after month. I wasn't sure how much more we could endure.

But there at the doorway almost immediately in front of me, my family, four important reasons to continue counting steps, to live.

Masks and Visions

I.

This is the mask of *Mamusia*
Who would come to America
If she didn't have to learn English
Pronounce in another language
the words *home, husband, farm.*

To name one's losses,
The ravens at the feeder,
Is to be shadowed by dark wings
Of death, take umbrage.

II.

This is the mask of death
That took her even after the operation
She did not want, her defiant glare
At the ceiling, the Polish radio droning.

War medals adorning her dresser.
One son lost, and missing from photographs.
Death, he came, and took them all
By surprise.

III.

This is the mask of the moon.
Forever looking after you
With a light that burns and burns
Through rooms and graves.

Pull this mask and you shall see
the hands of holy women
patient and unafraid.

Zofia

CHAPTER 4

Train Again (*Zofia*)

En Route South, Uzbekistan, 1941

STAY INSIDE while the men fight the cold walking to the frozen forest. Stay in the cabin and stay busy.

Cook a meal out of dried mushrooms and dried fish. If not so fortunate, improvise porridge again without using too much of the remaining flour. Pretend that it is all okay, that the porridge does not taste like glue.

Look Józef carefully in the eyes with a look that says "Don't worry, my youngest. We'll go home." It's not lying. It's survival.

Sweep, sweep, sweep. Keep the dust and thoughts away. Don't let the children know you are afraid. Keep time going, flowing forward and not back again to the farm, the lovely ripening trees bearing apples, plums and pears. Those delicate hours of tree-light and sun.

Sweep, sweep, sweep. There's a rhythm to keep time going so as not to stop and grow torpid, heavy with despair.

Time didn't pull as it used to on our farm, our orchards. Time used to pass swiftly. The children somehow grew up right in front of our eyes.

But now, time stopped. Growth stopped. Two interminable winters in Siberia had taken a toll on all of us.

At least it was finally summer, almost two full years after the War had started. Henryk and Helcia were in the forest picking blueberries and mushrooms that I would dry for next winter. Józef was still sulking because I wouldn't let him go with his older brother and sister. There would be a next winter we hoped, though we prayed not in Siberia. I wasn't sure we could survive another winter in the Arctic taiga. But somewhere, perhaps back on our farm in Poland... but Andrzej believed we would never return. He could not go through another deportation, another instance of being tied in front of his children. It was gambling, the Communists' deck stacked to win.

Andrzej missing behind his eyes, smoking his pipe, walking and looking nowhere. He had aged in the last eighteen months. We all had, I did not want to admit. Yet he the most. Helcia and Henryk acted more like adults than children. Their silliness, once embodied in Henryk's games and Helcia's songs, was truncated, left in a different life. Those former versions of ourselves lost.

School for the children was jerry-rigged. The children, who more so than usual as typical children in school, found it difficult to concentrate, yet were happy to be learning again, sitting in ordered rows, makeshift desks. Henryk missed the orchards and Helcia, her routine on the farm, singing hello to rooster, hen; her interrupted sixteen-hood; and Józef, too young to know. He was the luckiest or perhaps, the most scarred.

Every week, if possible, I had tried to barter an item of clothing, such as a pair of stockings, a pillowcase, a curtain, or whatever I could, in exchange for one or two pints of milk for Józef. On occasion I exchanged my sewing and mended a pair of pants or a coat for one of the local's children. The mothers understood how important this milk was for my youngest, and word traveled among them. If they weren't able to trade, they helped to find another woman who could. I was incredibly grateful for their empathy. I didn't feel like I was begging anymore, as the first time when I asked shamefully, unable to meet their glances.

Yes, Helcia and Henryk were somewhere in the forest picking blueberries and mushrooms. I was so tired, waiting for them to return. I swept the floor to stay occupied; the broom helped anchor me. I couldn't rest until I knew they were back safe. We would have mushroom soup for dinner and berries for dessert. I would dry most of what they picked for winter. They would be exhausted but happy with their harvest that would benefit all of us.

I couldn't help thinking about what would become of the children and how they would be able to thrive in the future after such negligible amounts of food. Helcia, who had planned to become a teacher of Polish literature and history, what options would she have now, taken out of formal school? And Henryk and Józef... I didn't know if I could cope if they were to choose the military like their father and grandfathers.

I heard strong footsteps hastening with an urgency outside the cabin. My stomach plummeted before my next heartbeat. Someone must be hurt, I feared.

Andrzej put his thin arms on my shoulders and looked

directly in my eyes as he had not done for many months. We all seemed to avoid one another's eyes as if they would disclose our thoughts. It was easier not to admit to them or ideally, not to think at all.

Why was Andrzej back early and studying my facial expressions? Something had happened to Henryk, I was sure. A mother instinctively knows. I felt dizzy and fumbled to sit at the bench next to the table.

The corners of Andrzej's mouth turned and there was a new look in his gray-flecked eyes. "Zofia . . . , " he paused, which frightened me even more. And then the words I prepared myself to hear, not coming close to imagining what they would be.

"Zofia, we're free!"

My first thought was that I must be dreaming. I must have drifted off again standing in front of the fire while starting the broth for the soup, overwhelmed by the heat. Perhaps too many months of hunger had triggered hallucinations.

Andrzej's words poured out quickly. I struggled to follow their path. I wasn't as astute as I used to be. It must be the lack of food compounded with unremitting stress.

He explained the good news: General Sikorski, head of the Polish forces in exile, had signed an agreement with Maisky, the Russian ambassador in London, announcing an amnesty for all Polish deportees. We were being "pardoned" suddenly. Stalin wanted to use Polish men (most of them military veterans) to help the Russian army fight the Germans who, despite the Molotov–Ribbentrop Pact, had attacked the Russians in June 1941. Sikorski asked General Anders, who had very recently been released from the Lubyanka prison in Moscow, to start amassing a Polish army in Buzuluk.

I was dumbfounded. "Are you sure it's not a trick?"

"Yes," Andrzej answered without hesitation, "it's been formally announced. It is not a trick but rather a different need for manpower for the War. A strategic shifting of alliances."

Andrzej decided it would be best for him to leave first with a group of men from our camp to join the Polish army assembling in Buzuluk. He was hoping that enlisting in the army would make it easier to get a furlough and come back for Helcia, Henryk, Józef and me. In the meantime, we were stranded without Andrzej, the head of the family, left to fend for ourselves.

We would leave a few weeks after him. We had to act relatively quickly before the Vychegda River froze so that we would be able to reach the town of Kotlas, which had the closest railroad station. We were too afraid to wait, to be trapped by the frozen river. Droves of shadows began emerging from the countless forced labor camps in an attempt to reach Buzuluk, in the southern part of European Russia where the first units of the Polish Army were to be formed.

The few remaining men in our camp organized a brief meeting. It was decided that all families would leave within two weeks and board a boat to reach the railroad station. This was agreed to be the best departure plan since there was a Polish liaison officer in Kotlas who could give us further instructions. We spent the next two weeks preparing—picking and drying berries and mushrooms, gathering anything edible, washing as many of our things as possible.

The river bank was ten miles away. For a few hundred rubles, the camp commander allowed a group of us to borrow several horses to transport our meager possessions to the bank of the river.

We waited for the next riverboat to get ourselves back to the town of Kotlas, to the railroad station where we had arrived eighteen months prior. In Kotlas the Polish liaison officer could provide more information and obtain Russian permission for us to join the train heading south. No, we would not be returning west towards Poland.

I didn't think we would make it out of Siberia alive, especially without Andrzej. But I understood why he had left. In his mind that was the best course of action to help his family as he had been unable to do for almost two years. Still, it was difficult without him. Even though Henryk stepped up to protect us, he appeared to be extremely boyish and thin. I probably appeared to be a frail, bereft widow. I often felt like we were easy prey.

I'm not sure what was worse: the eighteen long months in Siberia or the second train ride that consisted of many more days than our initial transport. We were crammed once again into cattle cars but this time without any help whatsoever from the Russian officials; there were no more rations of bread or warm soup. On this train ride, however, we had "freedom of movement," as the documents procured for us stated with their curving lines of ink and official Russian stamp. Before he left, Andrzej emphasized how important these documents were, instructing me to guard them carefully by sewing them inside the lining of my ragged coat.

"Amnesty," kept resurfacing in my mind, "a pardon for our crime." Our particular crime against the Russian state: being in the wrong place at the wrong time. Signed away by two leaders who drooled at the table of Poland with their gleaming carving knives. How I sounded like Helcia, one of her torn, hidden pieces of paper.

Twice as long on the train this time. I looked at Helcia's tally each day. At least we were heading south away from the Arctic cold and the men were relieved of their forced labor. Wherever the men were, I prayed they were well, alive.

The train did not follow any regular schedule; we never knew when it would stop or resume its journey. Often unexpectedly and without any announcement, the train departed earlier than previously stated—stranding many for long periods of time.

The train halted for a few hours or sometimes a few days; there was never any forewarning. On several occasions, the Russian officials pushed us onto the sideline where we would stay for two or three days. Other times, they would sideline us to let a military transport go by. Every time the train stopped people disembarked and cased the immediate vicinity to look for food. They would leave the train station and search throughout the neighborhood in an effort to buy, steal or barter for anything that was suitable for human or animal consumption. We were all terribly hungry and visibly gaunt. We dug in the soil for vestiges of cabbage, potatoes or onions from the prior year's crops.

After hunting for possible food to procure, eyes adjusting to the landscape scanned for a patch of level ground to build a small fire to heat water for soup or porridge. Everyone listened carefully for the whistle, or more often commotion, that announced the train's departure from the station and scrambled to board in time.

People desperate for food risked venturing from the station, only to be left behind when the train proceeded without notice. It was not unusual for a hundred people to be stranded without shelter. With any luck they would hop the next train heading south and catch up with the transport train in a day or two.

Helcia and a few others her age missed the train several weeks into our journey south. I was sick with anxiety, wondering if they would be able to meet up with the train, find an alternate form of transportation. What if the wolves... what if there were men... We had discussed quietly that being on the train was safer than wandering alone. Andrzej would locate us soon, I kept convincing myself and the children. "Keep looking for your father." Though I had to admit, I was pretty sure we would never see him again. Or maybe I was preparing myself for the worst.

Days and days of agony—of imagining what could be happening to Helcia and her friends. Afraid they would never catch up with our train. It had happened to others. They were missing for too many days to tally. Helcia may have been counting the days, but I could not. The days blurred with my fear that she, too, would never come back. So many elongated days elapsed. I had to resign myself that she was in God's care, if God were still paying attention to us.

After more than sixty days on the train, we were unloaded from the cattle cars onto the sandy banks of the Amu Darya River in Uzbekistan. The railroad authorities needed the train. Again, we were stranded like cargo.

While my eyes readjusted to the daylight, I forced myself to blink a few times. I couldn't believe it. Helcia! My oldest and only daughter was waiting on the banks of the river—relieved to be reunited with us. Somehow I expected to find the Helcia of the orchards; her thinness caught me off guard. I suppose she was an indication of how we all looked.

She apologized immediately, knowing that she had caused

worry. *Kochana* (my love), *remorse does nothing. You are back, you are safe.*

After the excitement of being reunited with us lessened, Helcia explained what had happened. Fortunately, several of her friends her age from the camp in Siberia were also stranded after the train left the station.

There were four boys and three girls who stayed together for almost three weeks until they caught up with the transport train. It was a lot easier and safer to travel in a group. Each had several rubles. They pooled their paltry resources and began hopping trains traveling in a southerly direction. Since they did not have proper documentation or tickets, they avoided passenger trains and opted for open platforms or wagons loaded with coal or other materials.

After they had spent the small amount of money, they started bartering from their layers of clothes since it was warmer heading south. Two of the boys wore halfway decent shoes, which they traded for four loaves of bread and a basket of mangoes in Tashkent, the capital of Uzbekistan. Several days later, they caught up with the transport at the banks of Amu Darya.

Józef clung to his sister, guarding her from another disappearance during the next three days while we waited for the barges that would transport us up the river. Several thousand of us were packed into two barges.

It was a particularly bleak journey. The unsanitary conditions prompted dysentery to spread rapidly through the overcrowded boat. The stench alone caused passengers to vomit profusely overboard. Every so often the tugboat pulled up to a small island in the middle of the river to jettison the dead. The men working on the boat simply threw the multitude of corpses overboard and the tugboat continued its slow course up the river. Out of respect we didn't stare at the bodies that floated behind the barges and would soon be completely submerged.

After several days the boat pulled up to shore. We were unloaded and divided into groups of forty to fifty people. Each group was sent to a different Uzbek kolkhoz, a collective farm controlled by the Soviet state, to work. A few families were crowded into a clay hut consisting of a single room with a dirt floor to sleep on. For food we roamed the nearby fields in hope of finding potatoes or discarded cabbage from the prior harvest. It was almost Christmas 1941.

It certainly didn't look like Christmas back in Poland or even in Siberia, where there was snow and an array of pine and fir trees. Here, several gray clay huts loomed in the middle of barren land without a single tree adorned with leaves or needles. Even the horses had a difficult time scaling the terrain for sustenance.

One brave Uzbek tried to cross a deep ravine in search of food, but his horse slipped on the rocks, broke one of its legs and had to be shot. Since the kolkhoz was not very large, the Uzbeks sold us two pounds of horse meat per family. After several trips to gather a large amount of tumbleweed to build a fire, we cooked the horse meat for several hours to no avail. The meat was as tough as rubber from a tire, but we were not about to waste the meat we had bought. We chewed each bite for five to ten minutes and eventually swallowed. It was a Christmas that none of us would ever forget.

I asked Henryk to gather more tumbleweed that was rolling down the foothills of the Pamir Mountains, so that I could make a few *blincy* from the last pound of flour we had brought with us.

A few weeks after our arrival in Uzbekistan, the first sign of typhoid struck practically all the people in our group. Out of seventeen people in our hut, five died within a week. It was commonplace to wake up in the morning with a dead body lying next to one of us. And with so many dying, it became difficult to separate the living and the dead. The dying afraid, clung to the living; the living afraid of being swept with them in death's undertow. It reminded me of pruning on the farm, cutting back dead vegetation so it wouldn't siphon the nutrients from the new growth and how, often, it was difficult to differentiate and separate dying and nascent growth. Often a newborn baby doesn't look quite alive until it is coaxed to start breathing.

Józef was the first in our family to be stricken with typhoid. We almost lost him in Uzbekistan; we took turns staying with him outdoors on a cement slab, praying that his 105-degree fever would lessen while applying wet cloths to his face. Soon, the disease took over all our emaciated bodies. All three of my children sick, it seemed, beyond repair. People were dying of typhoid everywhere around us.

We were all in the hospital January 1942. I kept reminding myself of the month and year as I often slipped back to the farm in Poland, days when the children were small and filled with laughter. Andrzej tossing them in the air and laughing. If only to go back to that time, those hours and savor them longer, study their intricacies better this time.

There was only one *arba* (a two-wheel vehicle that was pulled by a donkey) available to transport sick people to the hospital, approximately eight miles away. The donkey-led *arba* had to pass through a ravine to reach the hospital where it dropped everyone, quite literally. I don't remember how we climbed the twenty steps leading to the front door of the hospital that had quickly run out of beds. People were scattered in the hallways, under staircases, or wherever else there was room.

Henryk was unconscious for five days; Helcia suffered the most of any of us. She was unconscious for two weeks. Though emaciated too, as a young woman she had a little more body fat than Henryk, Józef or me. Consequently, the typhoid had something to feed on. From lying continuously on her back without being turned over, she lost most of the skin on her back, exposing several of her vertebrae which could be seen sticking out of her spine. Poor Helcia had lost most of her hair also. I was afraid she wasn't going to survive, but she smiled despite teary eyes and promised she would get well.

As soon as Helcia was able to stand up, we were discharged from the hospital with no place to go. We discovered very quickly that all of our shoes had been stolen. We had nothing to eat, no place to live. This was the worst moment of our entire stay in Russia. It could not get any worse. *Perhaps death would finally win.*

I looked up from this terrible thought and recognized a woman from our transport train. She knew that Andrzej wasn't with us. She pulled me aside from Helcia, Henryk and Józef to offer us floor space in a small clay hut that three Polish families rented from an Uzbek woman. "Yes," I answered her, "please," as I struggled to hold the water in my eyes before turning to the children to tell them our fortunate turn of events. I was grateful; it seemed like someone was watching over us—or perhaps, it was merely sheer luck. Either way, we were blessed somehow.

Several days later we learned that the Polish Army in the nearby town of Kitab was accepting young boys for a special Young Soldiers Battalion. The next day Henryk left to join that special unit in hope of obtaining additional food rations that he planned to share with us. He returned very discouraged. He was informed that the recruiting was not taking place until the following day. Determined to join and receive rations, he set off on the three-mile journey again early the next morning. I was proud of him, yet I mourned his boyhood. Józef had even less of one.

We stayed on the floor of the clay hut for more than two weeks, during which time Henryk walked three miles to visit us when he could, at least every other day, to bring us extra bread from his small rations. It was difficult to reconcile his adult behavior with his physical attributes of a starved boy.

We soon learned that General Anders had decided to move as many Polish deportees as possible immediately from Russian control while a window of opportunity existed. As a result of Anders' decision, Helcia, Józef and I were offered immediate transport by train with the Polish Army to Krasnovodsk, a port on the Caspian Sea—without having a chance to inform Henryk. He knew that the displaced civilian deportees would be repositioned separately, but nonetheless we felt awful leaving him without saying good-bye.

At Krasnovodsk, over three thousand of us scrambled onto the plank of a Russian freighter that had the capacity to carry only five hundred passengers. English soldiers distributed canned meat to the starved passengers boarding the boat. We walked ankle-deep in human vomit on the crowded deck, trying to reach the nearest point to be sick overboard, if possible. The conditions on the ship were deplorable, but the other side of the rough sea via the primitive, vomit-filled boat meant real freedom—away from Soviet influence. Because everyone's stomach was so empty and unused to food (not having eaten any meat for almost two years), many people died from the canned meat and never stepped off the ship alive. The British officials hired local men to bury the bodies of those who died aboard the ship in a sprawling cemetery on Iranian soil.

After three long days we completed the crossover to the port Pahlavi in Iran (Persia was renamed "Iran" in 1935, Helcia informed us). My oldest appeared livelier than I had seen her since our deportation; her hair was beginning to grow back. She was excited to be in the land of great poets and ancient stories such as "One Thousand and One Nights" and "The Conference of the Birds." She still remembered the translation of a Persian mystic's poem that she had memorized for school, and recited some lines from the ancient poet Rumi to Józef and me. A few other children and their mothers listened also as Helcia recalled from memory:

> One who has lived many years in a city, so soon as he
> goes to sleep,
> Beholds another city full of good and evil and his
> own city vanishes from his mind.
> He does not say to himself, This is a new city: I am a
> stranger here,
> No, he thinks he has always lived in this city and was
> born and bred in it.
> What wonder then if the soul does not remember her
> ancient abode and birthplace
> Since she is wrapt in the slumber of this world, like a
> star covered by clouds
> Especially as she has trodden so many cities and the
> dust that darkens her vision is not yet swept
> away.

The words captivated Helcia's audience and reminded us of the spiritual realm, of what we carried within. My daughter, perhaps she would become a teacher yet. The new glimmer of hope in her eye was contagious for all of us around her, though short-lived.

The Unholy Terror of Aloneness

The clenched ready to open. On the train,
in the hospital, glass eyes mirror
lost cities, stone echoes.

The bombs fell and then the pieces.
The orphan girl, *love her because she is
your link to the divine.* Her small fingers curl
around yours while you are not sleeping.
She, the lucky one, wakes without memory

If only. The emptiness only temporary
resurfaces to catch those moments
when you are a part. A link in the layers
found breathless or spoken.

At night, riding the train backwards
before the war confused with all of its arms.
The book you long to pick up.
Those pages beholden—a rapture of.

Uphill spin the story of phrases
unfurling secret codes, the flags shredded,
a jettisoned strategic plan, a *meta-logistics*.

We wait telling strange stories
of missing parts, lost connections.
How the general's plane never landed,
how the taiga is made of frozen glass.

Henryk

CHAPTER 5

Desert (*Henryk*)

Palestine, 1942–1947

THE LANDSCAPE was breathtaking in its heat and expansiveness. Beige and tan sand mountains of the desert enveloped us for an indeterminate number of miles. A parched landscape that rolled on endlessly. Its magnitude otherworldly, strange.

How do people live off such arid land? What possibly grows?

We were growing finally, it seemed. The sun's warmth and routine meals gradually began to heal the scars from the cold and from almost two years of hunger and disease.

When we arrived, we looked like skeletons webbed with taut skin. Emaciated to bone. The British soldiers' faces registered obvious alarm. They were expecting young soldiers, not scrawny boys whose uniforms were numerous sizes too large.

Our bodies were initially in shock: from taiga to desert; fifty degrees below zero temperatures to one hundred in the desert sun. But we didn't mind the heat. We were free to move about as we pleased, no longer starved prisoners.

Once again—far away from our homeland. Polish citizens without a country. Most of our fathers were fighting for our homeland somewhere unknown to us, fighting we all believed to keep Poland on the map with her own government.

We watched the Arabs under British control, the Jewish people without a nation either. Too many groups of people and not enough countries. The Arab women hidden under long black cloths, heavy suffocating drapes to keep women away from the world. They were always in mourning, it seemed, for a life of joyfulness and play perhaps, for books and freedom.

The desert. I was deserted . . . My father somewhere I did not know. Mama, Helcia and Józef sequestered from the War, safe, I hoped. I was no longer starving or cold, and wished the same for them. Would I see them again? Would I remember the details of Helcia's cerulean eyes and the touch of my mother's soft skin when I kissed her face? I recalled their images frequently to solidify them in my memory that seemed unable at times to distinguish between how things really were and how I remembered them or wanted them to be. That day in the orchards or in the forest hiding at night . . .

Alone, in the desert. A giant landscape for too many thoughts. Luckily there was order, training, school and tasks. While British troops took a siesta and remained in their tents from noon to two, the hottest hours of the day, my peers and I played soccer. These games helped bring our energy back and helped the time without a family or a nation, pass.

When our Young Soldiers Battalion reached Pahlavi by ship, the British soldiers stripped us to the bare bones; all clothing and earthly possessions were assembled into a huge pile, sprayed with gasoline, and lit on fire. Everyone was shaved. Men and women were shaved everywhere on their bodies and then led through a hot shower. This demeaning procedure was to ensure all lice and other insects were exterminated.

We emerged clean and hairless, a humiliating catharsis.

The British soldiers handed each one of us new underwear, uniforms, boots, hats and a blanket. Most of us could pull the trousers (that fell from our waists without a belt) up around our necks. The standard-size boots that had been issued were also at least two sizes too large, but nobody cared. After two years in Russian forced labor camps, we were finally free and had new, clean clothes, and shoes without rips or holes.

We stayed several days in the "tent city"; thousands of tents dotted Pahlavi's sandy beaches. We were then loaded onto large civilian trucks for a two-day trip to Tehran, the capital of Iran. The British commanders directed us to several empty hangars at the Tehran airport, which was vacant because of the War. The one blanket we each received served as a bed and pillow at night while we slept on the cement floor of the abandoned hangars.

For our meals we were required to march over a mile to the military refectory, located in the city's suburbs. Invariably there was only one menu for the entire two months we spent in Tehran, mutton in grease-saturated rice each day for every single meal. We were grateful for the regular frequency and sizeable portions of the meals, but after our stay in Tehran none of us ever ate mutton again nor could tolerate even the smell. Our stomachs were still adjusting to standard meals.

The damage to our health could not be immediately undone. It would take years, we would discover, to compensate for the conditions we had barely endured.

Increasingly, we began to regain some of our physical strength and also our mental capabilities. Every Sunday there was a celebration of Mass at the airport. In April a Polish bishop visited us to perform the sacrament of Confirmation. It was a military style of worship where over five hundred young men were confirmed in less than an hour. The sergeant stood in front of each platoon when Bishop Józef Gawlina confirmed us. After we each announced our chosen name for this rite, the Bishop blessed the entire battalion, making a single sign of the cross, "I confirm you in the name of the Father and the Son and the Holy Spirit. Amen." I chose the name Janek (John) as my Confirmation name out of reverence for St. John the Apostle, patron of books—in honor of Helcia, whose presence I craved. We were grateful for this sacrament that took place in public, something that could not have been possible under Russian jurisdiction.

During this time, Tehran developed into a large transit camp for the thousands of Polish deportees from Siberia. In addition to our contingent of approximately five hundred young military soldiers, there were three civilian camps for women and children as well as a field hospital to take care of the continuous string of new arrivals from Russia who were all severely malnourished and ill. Any time I saw or heard of new civilians in the area, I searched for Mama, Helcia and Józef. They were in one of the civilian camps, I hoped, but I didn't know for sure.

After about two months of rest, we were transported again in caravans, this time heading west toward Iraq. We were driven by local Iranian men who knew the intricacies of the landscape and studied us carefully from the rearview mirrors. Our first stop was the town of Kirkuk in northeastern Iraq. We said good-bye to our civilian drivers. From this point forth, our journey west toward Baghdad would be in the military half-ton trucks maneuvered by British soldiers.

Since 1942 the entire Middle East had been controlled by the British. The countries of Europe competed for lands in different continents, whereas my peers and I simply wanted a country of our own, Poland, again. The land of our fathers and grandfathers, the land bestowed for bravery. The land we would cherish and protect, grow old in, watch our own children evolve into adults some day. Or so we wished.

We rode in the half-ton trucks for several days until we arrived in Habbaniya, a transit camp situated on the shores of a large lake, approximately fifty miles west of Baghdad. We were to remain here for a fortnight, per British instructions.

The air temperature averaged 110 degrees Fahrenheit. An egg could be cooked in less than three minutes by merely being left in the sand. We were confined to our tents for the first three days because we did not have cork helmets, a mandatory piece of equipment in this scorching region. Leaving the tent without a cork helmet could cause heat stroke very quickly, in addition to a court-martial from the camp commander. The British soldiers brought food to our tents and emptied the pails that we used temporarily as toilets. It was a strange realization that expelling one's own waste privately was a missed luxury of sorts, though thankfully temporary.

Late on the third day the shipment of cork helmets arrived, finally allowing us to begin exploring the shores of the lake. We were surprised to see a body of water several miles long in the middle of the desert. It looked like a mirage. I thought I was in the hospital back in Uzbekistan merely hallucinating, or dreaming on one of our cattle car journeys. But the military uniforms reminded me that those months were over. I was sure Helcia would be able to describe this mirage eloquently on one of her ripped pieces of paper.

We were also mystified by the peculiar disappearance of aircraft as they approached the banks of the lake. Later, we learned that the British had concealed hangars under the large body of water. As soon as a plane touched down, the ground crew folded the plane's wings and rolled the aircraft into an underground tunnel, so it could not be seen by enemy air patrols. At first these sightings, too, did not seem real but rather another illusion of an exotic land. We also feared our minds were permanently affected from typhoid and from two years of chronic hunger.

One afternoon during our stay in Habbaniya, a group of eight of us went swimming to be relieved of the heat and to explore the area further. The landscape was completely different from the landscape of our homeland. The lack of trees made us feel more directly part of the universe and equally, more vulnerable. After a few hours of swimming and horseplay, the open skies dimmed and a sinister dark wall on the horizon raced in our direction. The skies completely blackened in a matter of seconds. Those closer to the shore successfully escaped the water, but two of our friends remained a substantial distance from the shore.

Realizing a khamsin (tropical sandstorm) was upon us, we yelled to them "Swim back!" One of the two heard our calls and managed to swim ashore. The other must have become disoriented and never made it back. Four long hours later, the sand blizzard finally subsided and we found his drowned body. He was fifteen years old, one year older than I was. When we buried him in the military cemetery, I imagined the whereabouts and details of his family who could not be notified. No one knew exactly where relatives were. Mama, I'm sure, agonized about Tata and me, not knowing if any harm had befallen us. I worried about my parents and siblings daily, praying they were all safe and that I would see them again.

We left Habbaniya after that tragic fortnight and continued our journey west towards Transjordan and Palestine, which was to become our next "home." The first camp, Bash-Shid, basically consisted of twenty acres of desert north of Gaza. There were only two army barracks amidst hundreds of tents. One of the barracks served as a kitchen and the other as the headquarters of the camp commander.

The objective of our cadre was to resume temporary schooling to compensate for the education we had lost. The conditions we found ourselves in were deplorable, however; unsuitable for even the most primitive resumption of an educational program. After a severe rainstorm most of the tents collapsed; the stakes anchored in pure sand popped up, unable to withstand the tension of the ropes. We spent the entire day repairing the tents and trying to affix them back in the sand more permanently.

After the intervention of our commanding officer with British high command, it was decided that we would move to another camp, Qastina, recently vacated by British troops. Here, the conditions were far from perfect—but a vast improvement over the first location.

It was in this camp that the sparse number of school officials gave us our first exam in an effort to place us into the appropriate class according to our educational and intellectual levels. Those showing the most potential were assigned to the Polish Army Cadet School, designed for training future Polish officers to replace the eight thousand officers who had disappeared without explanation in September 1939, shortly after the War began. Among several hundred young boys, I was selected to attend this prestigious school. I wanted to tell Helcia, Mama and Tata of my accomplishment, knowing how proud they would be, especially Helcia and Mama. My father would be proud also, but he would remain characteristically reticent, I knew.

I wondered if my parents and siblings were all healthy and had enough food to eat. Perhaps it was superficial to want to tell them of my school examination results. I would settle for a letter, knowing where they were, that they were all well, alive. I hadn't seen my father since the day he left Siberia with several other men to join the Polish Army—and Mama, Helcia and Józef since Uzbekistan; I didn't even have a chance to say good-bye. The last time I brought them extra bread, as I tried to do as often as possible, they were gone. I was sure they were on their way to better living accommodations, but the sudden reality of their departure left me acutely alone. I focused on school to forget about the indefinite absence and unknown whereabouts of my father, mother, sister and brother. I was a man myself after all, I kept telling myself, so that time passed somehow, one day blurring into the next, practically identical.

Our commanding officer secured the best possible teachers from among thousands of refugees who had shared our fate of deportation to Siberia. To make up for the loss of academics, we worked at an accelerated pace to complete two school years in one calendar year. The concentrated days of academics and military training passed swiftly. There was hardly time to think; we fell asleep as soon as we put our heads down. I often studied intensely and then shut my eyes to allow the information to ensconce itself. There were so many details and facts to memorize, categorize, and analyze on future exams. My brain felt rusty and feeble in contrast to its former capacity. School had been easy for me in Piłsudczyzna, but after months of not studying and not having enough food, it was difficult to concentrate and retain information.

After a year in Qastina our school relocated to yet another camp, Barbara, where we stayed for the next four years. Gradually our school consisted of six companies of four platoons each. Every platoon had thirty Polish cadets and formed a separate class. This school was incredibly well organized. The curriculum consisted of six hours of academics in the morning, followed by four hours of military training in the afternoon. Homework assignments had to be completed after dinner between six and eight o'clock in the evening. The school also had a very strong athletic program that included tennis, volleyball, basketball and soccer. Each company fielded a team that competed against other teams. Our regimental soccer squad played against British squads as well as local teams throughout the Middle East and Egypt. Often, on the soccer field, one of us was suddenly struck by the realization that while we competed for points, our fathers competed for more critical things—lives and the existence of our country, we believed.

In early 1943 it was rumored that before deployment to Italy, the Polish Army that had trained in Iraq for the last six months was scheduled to pass through Gaza, a town approximately six miles south of our camp. Many of us were hoping out of sheer fortuity to see our fathers, relatives, former schoolmates, or neighbors. I couldn't sleep the night before the predicted Polish Army stopover. I struggled to convince myself not to get my hopes up, but prayed that I would see Tata. My sleep was restless that night. I kept imagining that he would be in Gaza the next morning and that I would know what to say.

The next day a meeting didn't seem likely. Soldier after soldier, face after face, brought steady disappointment.

He was one of the last soldiers to arrive. I could tell he was tired but happy to see me. His eyes lit up immediately showing more emotion than I'd ever seen, as he was quintessentially stoical. My father in front of me was much older, more tired and appeared less invincible than how I had imagined him in uniform. He looked healthier than in Siberia, but more aged than I had visualized him in my memories and dreams. It was the Tata on the farm in Poland that I carried in my imagination, I realized. He, too, was probably grappling with discrepancies from his own recollections and anticipation.

The forty-minute visit with my father passed quickly, though we fumbled with what to say. I knew he felt guilty about leaving Siberia without us. He asked if I knew where Mother, Helcia and Józef were. I shook my head no, painfully conscious of how desperately he wished otherwise.

He explained that when he and the other men from our barracks in Siberia had finally reached Buzuluk, there was no one there. They were disheartened to learn that the Polish government-in-exile had changed the location for the recruitment base to Uzbekistan across the Ural Mountains. The absence of crowds of men at Buzuluk forced the realization that he would not be able to come back for us. His eyes filled, but he would not permit any tears to spill.

To break the uneasy silence, I narrated our own journey from Siberia to Iran. He again asked if when I left Mama, Helcia and Józef they were okay—given the circumstances.

No one could assume they were "healthy."

"Yes, they were doing well when I left them."

A British commander entered the tent where dozens of conversations between older and younger men took place hurriedly and almost inaudibly. The scene didn't seem real but rather a scene from a silent movie; mouths moving but no sound. The British commander's entrance signaled that it was time for the Polish Army to depart.

My father shook both my hands and patted me hard on the back in slow motion, it seemed.

"Take care, synu."

"You too, Tata."

The desert would become a memory like the mirage of the lake and British planes that disappeared under water. A film I would watch over and over again from afar. Our season of sun was a large stepping-stone where my fellow cadets and I grew and rested, bathed in heat, and forgot the long winters of hunger, disease and toil. The days were pleasant in the Middle East, but my peers and I knew this time of limbo would inevitably end.

Seasons of Rain and Sickness

The sequence of rain
speaks only of rain

erases piercing animal cries
those lost sleeping

skeletons in the forest
petrified against hemlock.

Waiting for the medicine-push
elixir without debilitating aftereffects.

Once liberated, the country
waits for literacy.

Greed another word for freedom's
occlusion
ancient indecipherable cause

called a coincidence
in accordance with genetic blueprints

a mistranslation of rain and fire.

Józef, Zofia, Helcia

CHAPTER 6

Mangoes and Grass Huts (*Helcia*)

Tanganyika, 1942–1948

THERE WERE two seasons in Africa, the season of Rain and the season of Scorching Sun.

Yes, there were two seasons: the season of War and the season of Forgetting.

The season of School and the season of Sickness.

The season of Books and the season of Malaria.

There was no Poland for us anymore, though Tata and Henryk both joined the Polish military in an attempt to reclaim her. We hoped they were well, alive. They could be somewhere in Iraq, Transjordan, Palestine, or anywhere the War took them really, especially Tata. Mama knew he could be fighting in the trenches again.

From Tehran, we were sent to Tanganyika, as it was called then. But as with other countries, its name, a symptom of ownership, would change. A country on the southeast perimeter of Africa where the British were in power politically and militarily yet prided themselves on their policy of "two-tier" rule. The indigenous people were allowed to govern themselves according to their complex system of tribal law, circumscribed and overseen by England. That, too, would change.

The most important Book of History was turning its pages

somewhere else with each day of the War. We were removed, taken aside, a mere appendix: "Displaced Persons."

The Africans stared at us, trying to figure out why we were there, who we were. If the British ruled over us, and why we were so thin.

A triangle of three: Mama, Józef and me—inside a larger group of women and children—tucked into mango and coconut groves. We prayed for Tata and Henryk every night. Mama was the loneliest, the most frightened; her eyes the most vacant. There was no school to take her mind off their absence and our uncertain fate—just daily chores in an attempt to create some sense of stability. For Józef and me, there would be studying again, eventually.

Yes, there were two seasons for us in Africa, the season of Torrential Rain and the season of Intense Sun that exposed flaws ruthlessly; cracks in the bone china, so to speak.

Our season of Winter was over. We missed Tata and Henryk, our home and farm. That other life seemed a mere dream in this new world of mangoes, red clay, and grass huts.

The Polish government-in-exile had decided to relocate the women and children who had been deported to Siberia to various places around the globe that were under British military protection. No one really knew where to put us. We couldn't go home—that area was under Stalin's control. The goal was to position us somewhere beyond the Soviet sphere of influence, where we could be protected by our British ally who was grateful for Poland's unfaltering military assistance. Poland was fighting for her own country, after all.

The largest group of Polish civilians from Siberia went to Africa, where there was room for Polish "refugees," as we were termed, though we did not leave our country by choice. The mothers of the group were terrified of what the extreme climate of Africa would do to their children who had already barely endured almost two years of brutal cold and hunger in the Arctic taiga and then critical cases of typhoid in Uzbekistan. Mama didn't have to tell us she was frightened; Józef and I sensed her apprehensions. We stayed near her when possible to circumvent the thoughts that haunted her solitude.

My baby brother was growing up despite the circumstances. He was seven years old but looked younger due to his height. Compared to Henryk at that age, Józef was very timid and uncommunicative in nature, which we understood to be the result of not fully comprehending the events he witnessed. Mama and I tried our best to coax him toward children his age whenever possible and asked him questions to entice him to speak. We explained that we were going to a new place that would be safe and exciting, where he would attend school again, eat plenty of healthy food, and grow tall and strong.

"But where is Tata?" he asked. "Will Tatuś be there?"

"No kochany (my love), but we will see him soon," Mama soothed.

It was the end of 1942 when we embarked from Tehran, almost three years since we were deported. Our long voyage to Africa by means of an archaic ship was deathly hot. We stopped to refuel at transit camps in Ahwaz, near Basra on the Persian Gulf, and Karachi, India, where we stayed for almost a week. I was so sick with tonsillitis and fever that I didn't even recall being in India.

Each voyage was convoyed by British naval units to guard us against Japanese submarines and aircraft. The journey was not only long but psychologically grueling for the adults; the children were resilient and excited about the new land where they would be staying temporarily, they were told, to regain their strength and compensate for the education they had lost. Subsequently, when we returned to Poland, they would immediately fit into their homeland, enroll in the proper grade, and carve out futures for themselves.

Despite the periodic rough seas and the prevalence of seasickness, the young children were fascinated by the new world of wall-to-wall ocean. They spent long periods of time staring at the water below, searching for creatures and colors beneath—ecstatic when dolphins arched from the water into the air to entertain them, they believed. The mothers on board sat on edge carefully watching to make sure no one, lured by curiosity, careened overboard.

A few of the British military personnel that accompanied us brought a map to the children, and outlined for them where the ship was, the exact latitude and longitude, from where we had originally embarked, and to where we were headed. We were grateful for these kind men who provided the young children with a fatherly presence. The only Polish male adults on the ship were elderly, whom we knew probably wouldn't survive the extreme temperatures in Africa very long. All the men the ages of the children's fathers had been recruited into the military. We did not speak about the War on this journey; it was enough for the children to confront another unknown land of temporary residence.

At night the tremendous expanse of stars captivated the children. They craned their necks back so their entire vision was a stage for the galaxies and perforations of light. It was difficult to get them to settle down and sleep. Those my age and older also admired the beauty of the open skies but like most of the mothers on the ship, we were more preoccupied with the uncertainty that lay ahead. Would the new land be dangerous? Would we starve and be sick again? Would we survive and be reunited with our fathers, brothers, husbands and sons?

We crossed the equator on the ship that would take us more than five thousand miles from Poland. "Five thousand," a number the children's intellects could not yet fathom. For the little ones, "Poland" also was a foreign concept since they were too young to remember the place of their birth. They were children of the earth, we told ourselves, who would once again fall in love with Poland. Their mothers told them of the beauty there, the trees and mountains, the villages of kind people, and sang them Polish songs to remind them of their culture. The entire deck remained silent as one mother sang a Polish lullaby to her three-year-old son:

Flows the Vistula, flows	*Płynie Wisła płynie*
Across the Polish countryside	*Po polskiej krainie*
She spotted Kraków	*Zobaczyła Kraków*
And will not bypass it.	*Pewnie go nie minie.*
Over my crib	*Nad moją kołyską*
Mother was bending	*Matka się schylała*
Teaching me	*I po polsku pacierz*
My prayers in Polish.	*Mówić nauczała.*

The background took on a dreamy, enigmatic quality as the African coastline appeared between spells of mist.

We had finally arrived at our destination for the time being—Tanganyika, ironically named by a British explorer in the native language of Swahili for sail (tanga) and bright arid plane (nyika). We disembarked from the ship at Dar-es-Salaam, a port city in the eastern part of the country. We were sent to a transit camp, Morogoro, that was not completely ready for our habitation. The huts we were to live in, quite rudimentary and hastily built, provided some shelter from the climate and wildlife. The roofs rested on poles and the walls were made of thick layers of elephant grass, named for its mammoth size.

Mama, Józef and I shared a hut with another Polish woman and her daughter who was a few years older than Józef. They also had a farm in eastern Poland and Polish military affiliations. Her husband was one of the military officials who disappeared without explanation immediately after the War began. Instead of Siberia, their village had been sent from Poland to Kazakhstan. She narrated how they dug their housing as many meters underground as possible in an attempt to stay warm since there was a shortage of wood to keep fires burning. Most of them froze to death. Although our conditions in Siberia had remained harsh, at least in the taiga we had an abundance of firewood to keep us alive.

In Africa, the line between the outside, natural world and the human, inside world was very tenuous at first, especially in our preliminary shelter in Morogoro. The jungle surrounded the camp and created an aura of intrigue and at night, fear. There were noises of wild birds, rhinoceroses, packs of dogs and hyenas, native drums, and ritual cries. Józef was afraid at first but quickly acclimated to the sounds and sights of this new, foreign land.

This was the first time we had seen dark-skinned people. The indigenous people were mostly of Bantu and Masai origins. The men carried spears at all times, and the tall women balanced jugs on their heads to transport water and food. Curious yet shy, they examined us too, especially our eyes and hair. They were quite elegant, I thought, with their lean lines and graceful movements in their native land, where they seemed to adapt to the landscape effortlessly instead of dominating the natural world.

A few weeks after our arrival in Morogoro, just when the children were settling down into their new surroundings, there was a terrible jungle fire near us that the adults knew threatened our safety. The thin stream at the western periphery of our camp didn't seem wide enough to hamper the raging fire. Scorching flames swallowed trees; the screeching of burning wild animals pierced the night. I would never forget those horrific sounds, the desperate wails of pain, and all of us unable to do anything to save those animals. We couldn't help but wonder how we would save ourselves, prevent such human wailing.

We were incredibly lucky; the fire was not able to jump the stream. But it was hard to sleep that night. Images of animals aflame haunted me.

Several weeks after the horrible night of fire, we realized an outbreak of malaria had permeated the camp, infecting almost every one of us. Most of us suffered from debilitating headaches and lethargy. Mama, Józef and I all had the strain of malaria that had infiltrated our camp as quickly as the wild fire had razed the jungle. The chronic disease carried by mosquitoes would return intermittently for our entire stay in Africa. The doctor at the camp prescribed quinine, a bitter-tasting drug made from cinchona bark; it treated the symptoms but did not eradicate the disease that caused anemia and exhaustion. Each dose, a gummy brown tablespoon of mud, tasted awful. It was difficult to swallow the thick medicine and then not to vomit.

Because the majority of us were stricken with the disease in this camp, we were moved to a different location, Camp Ifunda, much higher in elevation and not infested with malaria-carrying mosquitoes. The daily dose of quinine eventually kept the malaria from worsening, and the throbbing headaches subsided in Ifunda.

The elevation of this second camp also created cooler, more pleasant living conditions than in Morogoro. The only schools in this second camp, unfortunately, were grammar schools to accommodate the young children who comprised the majority of the Polish population. Fifteen girls around my age and I were sent to a different camp, Camp Tengeru (the largest Polish settlement camp in Tanganyika) to attend high school. All the boys our age had been recruited into the Polish military. The fifteen girls and I lived in a section of the large orphanage in Tengeru for three years while our mothers and younger siblings remained in Ifunda, allowing the grade-school children to attend better grammar schools. During holidays from our studies, my teenage peers and I traveled two hours by bus back to Ifunda to visit our mothers, younger brothers and sisters. Józef always wanted me to stay and couldn't understand why I lived apart from him and Mama.

Beyond our academic instruction, the sixteen of us basically fended for ourselves at this camp. We were responsible for washing and mending our clothes. Fortunately we shared the food that was prepared for the orphans from the fresh produce of the camp farm. There was no dining hall; we ate where we slept and studied. We each stored our minimal personal belongings neatly next to our single beds. We were in one section of the orphanage that was managed by several "room mothers." The children in the Tengeru orphanage were doing remarkably well under the women's supervision. It was relatively quiet for one space with so many parentless children; it took months for their youthful spirits to return.

There was one radio at the camp. Members of my small high school class were assigned different time slots to listen to the radio, take notes, and report back what was going on in the War that seemed fantastically detached from the structured life at our camp. We were removed from the world essentially.

In total, there were twenty-two large Polish settlements in Africa that provided shelter for approximately nineteen thousand Poles. Children and young people encompassed more than half the population. It was a challenge to open enough elementary schools to accommodate them and to provide the required teachers and textbooks. Luckily, food was in abundance, unlike in Siberia, and we were not under hostile command. Originally the settlement camps were designed to be convalescent centers to restore our health after Siberia and Uzbekistan. We suffered long-term physical and psychological repercussions from the diseases and hunger we barely had lived through and the multitude of deaths we had witnessed at close range.

The first year in Tanganyika there had been no formal classrooms; classes were conducted in barracks that resembled horse stables. The children grew a bit restless and bored inside, though the landscape and its animals intrigued them.

It was quite common to catch sight of a gazelle, antelope or rhinoceros. Many of the children were unruly that first year, until they were able to settle down into a routine and fully trust their teachers and the other adults in the camp. For many, the future was uncertain and bleak. Traumatized by their past that they were not old enough to fully understand, like Józef, they remembered fragments on visceral levels instead of logical plateaus. They were afraid of war and prayed nightly for peace, for the soldiers all over the world to return to their homes and families. Many asked their teachers and guardians how people could kill other human beings. Wasn't God watching?

Most of the women and children brought to Africa were the families of former farmers from eastern Poland, and therefore the percentage of educated people remained scant. There were over eight thousand Polish children enrolled in school. After an initial diagnostic evaluation, chosen advanced students deemed mature enough and psychologically capable were allowed to skip a grade level. There was also an accelerated program for the students who could keep up with a fast pace; a year of academics covered in six months.

Classes were conducted primarily in Polish with English as a mandatory second language. I had no knowledge of English until I attended school in Africa. The school day in Tanganyika ranged from six to eight hours and included Saturdays. During severe tropical storms, classes would frequently have to be cancelled. The sounds of the heavy rains were soothing, lulled my overtiredness into sleep, and seemed to wash away dusty thoughts, disturbing fears, and the haunting flashbacks of our deportation, cattle car rides, days of starvation and disease.

The hours and days of heavy rains and sleep encompassed a different time and place of restoration and forgetting. The days lost during the rains, however, would be made up on

Sundays and evenings to cover the condensed material of our programs. But I didn't mind. It was worth having those days of deep, curative sleep that cleansed the gray residue that had settled on my worn-out thoughts.

Each camp developed gradually over the initial year or two into a semi-autonomous microcosm. There were communal dining halls in most camps and eventually small churches, infirmaries, recreation centers, schools, a theatre, garden area, cemetery, and in some camps even a small hospital.

The front entrance of all camps was guarded by an *askari* (police officer), to regulate the comings and goings of people in and out, which created a sense of order and safety. Retired British army officers were in charge of the camps at the highest level but left the general administration to the Polish "settlers." Working beyond the camp was strictly forbidden. The Polish government-in-exile in London did not favor the permanent dispersal of Poles; the intention was that all those temporarily relocated would return to Poland immediately after the War.

The landscape was brown in the sun-scorched lowland areas and lush in the more tropical areas. Planted in geometric order, the tropical orchards included a wide range of cacti and succulent fruit, mango, papaya, coconut, and banana trees. After our time in Siberia, these trees of ripening fruit seemed to loom in lush paintings or in the dream world. Several times I touched the fruit or leaves to assure myself that the trees were real. Nearby there were coffee and sugarcane plantations and a view of the snow-capped mountain of Kilimanjaro. There were such radical extremes in this new land—extremes of dryness and lushness—burning sun and snow-capped mountains—the dark skin of the people of the land versus the light skin of the

European "visitors"—the natives' dire poverty and the wealth of the English and Hindu merchants—hovels juxtaposed with mansions.

The teachers planned sight-seeing excursions when possible to keep the children preoccupied and motivated, excited about learning in the actual world. The children were able to observe a variety of animals and plants in the wild that they would have never been exposed to. They visited Kilimanjaro and Nairobi, which was considered the capital of Eastern Africa at that time; their teachers incorporated assignments into these field trips. Scouting, established in Poland in 1910, also became an important sphere of the children's lives that helped inculcate their cultural identity and provide a sense of purpose. The Polish scouts had their own newspaper and emphasized living an ethical and useful life that contributed altruistically to the world. The scouts' oath affirmed service with one's whole life to God, Poland, fellow human beings, and to the scouts' law that emphasized living responsibly with an attitude of friendliness, honor and respect for nature and one's neighbors.

Two Polish newspapers, the weekly *Głos Polski* (The Voice of Poland) and the bi-weekly *Nasz Przyjaciel* (Our Friend), printed in Nairobi, circulated throughout the Polish populations. The Polish Red Cross had an office in Nairobi, also. We hoped this organization could reunite broken families by verifying whether relatives were alive or dead and if alive, locate their whereabouts and facilitate correspondence to reestablish communication. I wrote a short letter to Henryk and to Tata and sent both in care of the Red Cross in Nairobi. My letters informed them of where we were living, that Mama, Józef and I were all well, and asked to hear from them about their health and location. I ran to check the mail delivery for months but received no replies to my letters.

Time somehow passed in these settlement camps. Radio broadcasts officially announced the end of the War on August 15, 1945—Japan's surrender crystallized after the American attacks on Hiroshima and Nagasaki. I was stunned by the new weaponry, the atomic bomb, though grateful that the War had finally ended. The aftermath proved anticlimactic, however; our lives went on the same. We couldn't return to Poland: it was not a "free state." Because we refused to return immediately, we were stripped of our Polish citizenship. Officially we had no country, no homeland, no government protection of human rights.

I was the one who heard the upsetting radio broadcast at the beginning of June 1946. Members of the Polish military were asked not to march in the celebratory Victory Parade in London on June 8th; those in power in England and the United States did not want to alienate Stalin. Seething with anger, I wondered if this detail, this omission, would find its way into history books: all the Polish lives sacrificed for the Allies' cause—and no recognition or assistance in reinstating a free Poland under its own rule.

I was walking around the camp with a classmate one evening when one of the headmasters approached me and asked if I would be willing to teach Polish history and litera-ture to the incoming group of high school children. I had just passed my junior college exams with solid marks, which was a surprise since chronic fatigue prevented the extensive studying I had planned. Despite my exhaustion from having malaria for so long, I knew how difficult it was to find qualified teachers for the schools in the Polish settlements and could not refuse. The quinine that I took each day kept the malaria from progressing, but I was chronically fatigued as were so many others at the camp.

I knew the children were in desperate need of teachers, so I accepted the teaching position and struggled with my waning levels of energy. The students required a vast amount of instruction and guidance. I often fell asleep while grading assignments well into the hours of night or sometimes the early hours of morning with the kerosene lamp aflame. How I longed to work around the clock to prepare their lessons and grade their assignments. My mind wasn't as sharp as it should have been, impeded by the years of various sicknesses— pneumonia, typhoid, typhus, malaria—and starvation.

At the end of 1947 the International Refugee Organization pressured for the closure of the Polish settlement camps in Africa that had been designed for safety and asylum during the War. The women and children who had husbands, fathers or brothers in the Polish Army qualified as the first to leave. Persistent letters from surviving parents in Poland, much to the chagrin of almost everyone in the camp, encouraged the small number of half-orphans to return to Poland, which we knew was not the same place we had left. Other letters from eastern Poland, illegally incorporated into Russia, described how the Russian government had confiscated the farmers' cattle for the community farm and garnished heavy taxes to be paid in produce, approximately half of all crops. The orphans whose parents had both died were sent to various locations away from Poland, such as Mexico, Australia, New Zealand, India and Canada.

I could not believe that our time in Africa was finally drawing to a close and that we would not return to Poland. We had all realized for quite some time that a homecoming was unlikely, but now that roadblock was painfully vivid and insurmountable. We were scheduled to take a plane to England and would probably never set foot in Poland again. Unlike the orphans, at least I had some of my family with whom to build a new life.

I couldn't imagine what it was like for the children in the orphanage who were to be transplanted again somewhere, without parents, without family, without a clear nationality and homeland. I had grown especially fond of one of these orphans, my student Magdalena. She was enamored of poetry and words, as I had once been. I prayed that, unlike me, she would stay enthralled, that history and her own experiences would not erode her zeal.

On the day Mama, Józef and I were leaving for Nairobi via truck for the plane to England, I visited Magdalena to say goodbye. I handed her a parcel wrapped in a Polish newspaper tied with a piece of string. I asked her to open the package after I had left; she nodded that she understood. It was the dictionary that my teacher had given me back in Poland, that I had hidden in my belongings February 10, 1940 when the Russian soldiers commanded that we leave our home.

Pieces of pages had been ripped out of the dictionary—the blank margins on which I had written fragments of poetry so long ago. There were tallies of days on the train, days lost, and words underlined: *głód* (hunger), *męstwo* (fortitude), *nadzieja* (hope), *naród* (nation), *rozpacz* (despair), *śimierć* (death). I had written a small note to her inside:

To Magdalena (Tanganyika, Africa—July 1948),
a beautiful, intelligent child of this earth.
Stay lovely, inspired, kind—
in love with history, language and poetry.

*With affection and sincere good wishes for the future
in which God will bless you.*

Your teacher,
Helcia Jopek

[D]ANGER: to live in a place not one's own.

The sickness cannot be measured properly
choking sleep, ironing belief into *this* and *that*.

Papers folded and refolded until they disappear.
All traces. Lost bits filling in the lids of sleep

The horizon of fatigue only disturbed
by hunger. The nervous system,
a house of cards, and wind again.

A woman pleads with her child to
grow again, you must.

The war goes on in back rooms
where only men are allowed to tell their stories
do what it is they say they do and swear
it will never happen again

Villains can change out of costume,
spectators, easily cajoled
the cartographer obsequiously pleasant
to be paid on time.

Bodies undug and reburied
teeth tied in frayed felt
giving over one darkness
for another.

Monte Cassino

CHAPTER 7

Shrapnel (*Andrzej*)

Uzbekistan, Italy, the Middle East, 1941–1947

ZOFIA, HELCIA and Józef in the window beyond the snow—
their image receding, my world-worn Madonna of Częstochowa.
The farm gone again.
Over and over, I watch the Russian soldiers take everything
away—our land, our house, our livestock, our lives.

What does Helcia's tiny piece of paper say? I can't bring the
lines of her script into focus.
The lines transform into insects swarming all over our skin
when the kerosene lamps are turned down.
Counting steps, counting trees.
Counting bullet holes.
Too much time waiting alone. Without Zofia, Helcia, Henryk,
Józef.
Did I make the right decision to leave Siberia with the other
men without our families?
How long can a man sit back and watch his offspring and
spouse starve?

Our fathers would have praised our bravery (had they lived)
as would our sons if we would ever tell them. But to speak of war

diminishes its magnitude. Language cannot accurately describe the terror of enemy fire, tanks approaching, grenades, land mines. Words tarnish the already-clouded moments, unreal.

Single file to the train after being tied helpless in front of one's wife and children, the ultimate purloining: of a man's stance, ability for action. Cut those moments out and bury them—to be excavated and relived only privately.

Rip the pages out of Helcia's dictionary and set them on fire. The way books claim certain atrocities never happened.

The journey from Siberia was brutal. It took several months to reach Buzuluk, west of the Ural Mountains, near Kuibyshev. Hundreds of men congregated in train stations hungry, waiting days at a time for transport. No one identified us as soldiers since we did not have uniforms. I'm sure everyone assumed we were a group of vagabonds or beggars due to the state of our clothing and the gauntness of our faces and limbs.

Many of the men fleeing the forced labor camps died from dysentery, typhus, pneumonia or starvation during the journey. Finally free, but too late. Buried with unmarked graves in a cemetery next to a transit camp.

It was difficult to believe that we had "freedom of movement" finally, but the travel document stating so was tangible, on me at all times.

When we finally reached Buzuluk, we learned that the Polish military recruitment had been moved across the Ural Mountains to Uzbekistan, approximately twelve hundred miles away. My plans to obtain a furlough and go back for Zofia, Helcia, Henryk and Józef disintegrated.

We rested one night in Buzuluk, exhausted and frustrated, and then began our journey to Uzbekistan. There were seventy thousand Polish deportees in Buzuluk to join the Polish military, and food rations for a little more than half of us.

Churchill had convinced Stalin that the Polish former forced laborers, many of whom were military veterans, could be better utilized to fight the common enemy. Stalin agreed to the strong recommendation, but wanted the Polish troops to be absorbed into the Red Army. General Sikorski, the head of the Polish forces in exile, did not agree with the Russian plans and appointed General Anders to assume responsibility. Anders formed a fully independent army to serve under the command

105

of the Polish government-in-exile. After British and American pressure was placed on the Soviets, they agreed to this discrete formation of Polish forces. The Soviet Union shifted from captor to ally, though it was an "ally" we would never trust.

General Anders negotiated with Stalin to evacuate the Polish deportees from Kazakhstan, Uzbekistan, and the south of Russia around the Caspian Sea. The argument was made that if Russia released the Poles, the Soviet government would no longer have to feed and clothe the deportees.

Approximately one hundred twenty thousand Polish expatriates, including seventy-five thousand soldiers under Anders, were evacuated from Uzbekistan to Iran. The remaining able-bodied men who did not arrive in time to be evacuated, as evacuations were halted in August of 1942, were required to join General Berling's brigade that later fought alongside the Red Army.

I was grateful to be in the first contingent and not the latter. After I finally joined the Polish Army officially, we began a limited training period, those of us who were able to march or at least stand. We were given British uniforms; eventually Polish emblems that depicted a fir tree and "Poland" in large, white letters on a red background were sewn on the upper sleeve. Ill-equipped for this regimen, many Polish men died during those initial days. Despite the continuing deaths, many of us persevered through several months of intensive training supervised by British military instructors.

After the gradual rebuilding of our physical and mental strength, the top command started the separation of soldiers into what would later become known as the formation of the Second Polish Corps, consisting of armored brigades, an artillery group, a cavalry regiment, sapper and communications battalions, auxiliary services, and two infantry divisions, the Third Carpathian and the Fifth Kresowa. The First Polish Corps had been organized in England during 1940 following the evacuation from France, as France was falling to the Germans.

We were told that the women and children of military families from the Soviet labor camps had been transferred south of Russia to India and Africa to convalesce away from the War. Zofia, Helcia and Józef were either in India or Africa, if they had escaped Siberia alive. I prayed they were safe, no longer hungry and in sanitary conditions finally. Every night on my knees, I prayed that I would see them again. I shouldn't have left them, I feared. Henryk had probably enlisted in the Polish Young Soldiers Battalion that we heard about from the commander. He was too old to be considered a child like Józef but too young for the regular army. I prayed that Józef was still with Zofia and Helcia.

From Iran the Polish Army was moved to Iraq where we underwent six months of intensive training before our deployment to Italy. En route to Alexandria, Egypt we stopped in Gaza. The Polish Army Cadet Corps was located six miles away at Camp Barbara.

Many of us hoped that we would see our sons. I tried not to count on such luck, but the excitement of the other men proved contagious.

The vast landscape of the desert so unlike Poland and Siberia. It was literally breathtaking: difficult to breathe in the sudden heat. Nothing around for mile after mile—except for sand, sun, and the wind's etching of patterns upon hot grains of earth.

After learning that the Polish Army would stop in Gaza,

a large group of Polish cadets had gathered at the railroad station hoping to see their fathers.

Henryk in front of me for approximately forty minutes that didn't seem real; a reel I would replay over and over, why didn't I say such and such?

Henryk in a uniform, carrying a gun, marching as a soldier, studying me with reservation, not knowing what to say.

How could I have left them?

We parted awkwardly, both of us aware that we would not see each other for a long time, if we were fortunate enough to see each other again. I remember shaking both his hands before I patted him solidly on the back. My oldest son, my connection to Zofia, Helcia and Józef.

The Second Polish Corps, a total of one hundred ten thousand men, traveled to Alexandria and from there, we were shipped to southern Italy. We were annexed to the British Eighth Army in December of 1943 and stationed along the Sangro River line to gain combat experience in this War. Many of us had front-line experience from twenty years prior but were considered rusty. The weaponry had changed. And we were older, our reflexes slower.

So much for my plans to live out the rest of my days on our farm and never step foot in a war zone again. The last time in the trenches when I was in my early twenties, I had pleaded with God for a simple, peaceful life. I promised to be a good man in return. Now I prayed to be reunited with my family and never to witness war again.

In mid-April we relieved the Allied troops who had sustained a high number of casualties while trying to open the road to Rome. The Allied forces had been stuck since January, unable to break through the Gustav line. The British high command wanted to use the Second Polish Corps as a replacement pool of soldiers. The number of casualties was very high, especially for the New Zealand troops. The Polish command finally convinced the Allies to allow the Poles to fight as a unit, to preserve our military organization and identity.

Following confidential orders, the Allies launched a massive artillery barrage on May 11, 1944 that began yet another battle for Cassino, code-named "Operation Diadem." The ultimate goal of this battle was to capture the monastery at Monte Cassino and the surrounding hills, break through the Gustav line, and open the road to Rome.

My company, the 505 Transport Company of the Fifth Infantry Division, was tasked with delivering ammunition to the troops engaged in the battle for Monte Cassino. Soldiers of the Second Polish Corps secured portions of the blood-spattered hills. German paratroopers launched counterattacks in an attempt to throw the Polish soldiers off the hill. On May 12th we were ordered to breach positions held by elite German paratroopers.

It was during one of my trips back from delivering ammunition to the foothills of Monte Cassino that a blast from artillery shells exploded without warning. My supply truck lurched off the path and rolled more than a hundred feet down into a gully. The last thing I remembered was the unbearable, excruciating pain on the left side of my head and everything turning white at once—glaring intense light reflected against metal, blinding my last moments of consciousness with an unbearable brightness—and then a thick door slammed shut or a switch turned off: sealing absolute darkness.

I regained consciousness two weeks later in a British hospital in Italy, my head in bandages. A doctor, with the help of a Polish nurse who translated, described the details of my injury: a grenade had exploded near my truck and shrapnel hit the left side of my head through the window of the driver's side. A soldier in the truck following me extricated my body before my vehicle caught fire and radioed for immediate medical assistance.

I listened carefully to this information, but longed to know the result of the battle. The British doctor answered that the Second Polish Corps had taken the monastery at Monte Cassino, proudly staking the Polish flag on May 18th atop the rubble and debris of stone and flesh. The Polish nurse was smiling throughout her translation while tears streamed her face. Elated that we had won such a critical battle that had taken so many lives, I pictured the red and white Polish flag waving tenaciously. I attempted to smile, so that the doctor and nurse knew I understood their words, but I couldn't will my face to move.

Am I paralyzed? I asked.

No, feeling should come back. Time will tell.

Much later I was to learn the heavy price that the Polish Army paid for its triumph at Monte Cassino: almost one thousand Polish soldiers were killed and over thirty-five hundred wounded. The victory was the major breakthrough of the entire Italian campaign. Radio broadcasts reported that General Anders received numerous congratulatory telegrams from the British and American top commanders. Feliks Konarski, one of the soldiers fighting for Monte Cassino on the eve of the ultimate battle, composed a poem that would become one of Poland's national anthems (banned in communist Poland), "Czerwone maki na Monte Cassino"

("The Red Poppies on Monte Cassino"):

> Red poppies on Monte Cassino,
> Instead of dew, drank Polish blood.
> As the soldier crushed them in falling,
> For the anger was more potent than death.
> Years will pass and ages will roll,
> But traces of bygone days will stay,
> And the poppies on Monte Cassino
>
> Will be redder having quaffed Polish blood.

> *Czerwone maki na Monte Cassino*
> *Zamiast rosy piły polską krew...*
> *Po tych makach szedł żołnierz i ginął,*
> *Lecz od śmierci silniejszy był gniew!*
> *Przejdą lata i wieki przeminą,*
> *Pozostaną ślady dawnych dni!..*
> *I tylko maki na Monte Cassino*
>
> *Czerwieńsze będą, bo z polskiej wzrosną krwi.*

Every time I heard this song I was brought back to the Italian hills and something inside me avalanched swiftly, causing everything to dim.

I stayed in the hospital for five months and underwent several surgeries to remove as much shrapnel as possible. I was told that it was a miracle that I had survived and that my injury was not complicated by infection. The British nurses would not allow me to look at my face despite my repeated pleas and assurance that I would not be discouraged.

Let more days pass; let time heal. The body mends itself more quickly than we think.

Somehow time did pass in between blurs of memory and strange dreams. In nightmares, I visited various war zones. Everything was distorted by smoke and confusion. I reached for ammunition, but there was none. Soldiers were missing hands; limbs were missing civilian bodies. There were limbs in the trees, a severed foot still inside a worn shoe.

In the less frequent, intermittent dreams, I was at home in Poland, on the farm or a young child with my parents ambling through the fields. Under the sun, warm—holding someone's hand. Sometimes Józef's; sometimes my mother's. Sometimes Zofia was with me. One detail remained constant upon waking: an overwhelming sense of confusion of where I was and then the acute knowledge that I was alone.

I prayed Henryk was not involved in any combat and that Zofia, Helcia and Józef were safe and not compromised by despair, that abstract entity that wielded such determining powers with magnetic force.

My military career was over, at least combat duty. After the five long months in the hospital, I was regaining my health but my muscles had atrophied. It took several weeks to learn to walk again. I counted the painful steps, determined to increase my number each time. I struggled to remember how I had walked the thousands of steps in the frozen taiga; Henryk walking behind me. *Don't let him see any fatigue or hesitation.*

Ten steps, such a marvel. I would never have to march again. I would never walk through my orchards. But I would walk. Despair would not claim me. Not now. My family, though

I didn't know where they were exactly, I believed unequivocally, still needed me.

When I could finally walk twenty steps on my own, the Polish top command dispatched me to the Middle East away from the front line, and I was assigned the job of military chauffeur for a Polish colonel. I hoped Henryk would still be there in Gaza with the Polish cadets. It was October 1944, almost two years since my unit had stopped near his camp on our way to Italy. I had no more sense of time; it was not consistent. Time was an accordion compressed and expanded by a higher power; now a waltz, now a dirge, now a frenetic melody.

When my oldest son recognized me, he looked stunned, and stared at the scar marking my face from the left side of my head down to my jaw. I explained the accident and my recuperation. Henryk remained silent, grateful that I was alive.

"What about Mama, Helcia and Józef?" I asked.

"Nothing yet. The Red Cross is still trying to find them."

My tent was located near a weapons pool, not far from the barracks that served as classrooms for the Polish cadets. Henryk studied in those classrooms; in addition to the main curriculum of mathematics, physics, Polish, English, Latin, history and geography, his matriculation diploma would span thirteen subjects in all.

Despite being well-fed, the cadets were young, growing men ranging from fourteen to seventeen years old and were always hungry. I made it a point to bring some spare food from the officers' mess hall to make an extra sandwich for Henryk. He had a longer break between two classes and would run up to my tent knowing there was food for him there in a cooler. I was proud of him. He had transformed into a young man and was still obtaining the highest grades in all his classes. He was intelligent. I did not want him to be a soldier for the rest of his life.

On August 15, 1945, a radio broadcast announced that the War had finally ended. There was cheering everywhere—in the background of the broadcast, in the streets of London, under the desert sun. The dirge became a cacophonous pastiche of sounds. The Allied Forces had the last word, leaving Japan with no choice but to surrender after the employment of such horrific, modern weaponry. We could go home theoretically. Though home would not be Poland, not unless we wanted the Russians to determine our fate again. Russia. England. America. Stalin, Churchill, Roosevelt—a triumvirate that sealed our fate at the Tehran and Yalta conferences. A triangle that would exclude the welfare of other nations; their separate angles comprising one whole.

Nothing changed for us very quickly, aside from the Jewish unrest that intensified each month. Our experiences in Poland made us sympathetic to the plight of the Jewish population fighting for an independent state of Israel, their desire for a country, a homeland. The British realized it was time to withdraw their forces from the region and from the entire Middle East. Since we were under British command, all the Polish military personnel and civilians were required to leave also.

We boarded yet another train headed for Alexandria, Egypt. A ship was waiting for us to sail the length of the Mediterranean Sea via the Straits of Gibraltar, where General Sikorski's plane had perished on July 4, 1943—twenty seconds after the plane had taken off. Most of us suspected retaliation against Sikorski for exerting international pressure on the investigation of the mass graves in the Katyń forest that Nazi Germany discovered in 1943.

The estimated twenty-two thousand of those executed in the Katyń massacre included the approximately eight thousand Polish high-ranking officers who had mysteriously disappeared in 1939. The Soviet Union vehemently denied any role in the deaths of the bodies (unearthed by the Germans), most of which had been shot efficiently with one bullet in the back of the head at the perimeter of the mass grave that the victims had been commanded to dig for themselves. Since the Soviet Union remained a British and American ally, connection to this massacre would taint the Allied forces. Russia blamed Germany vociferously. And Sikorski's fatal accident was publicly deemed bad luck.

Out of the 1.5 million Polish deportees from 1939–1940, only one hundred and twenty thousand were saved by General Anders by way of Iran. The highest percentage had died, many were relocated, some were nationalized as Russians, and a small group chose repatriation to Poland after the War.

I knew Henryk and I were lucky to be alive. We would begin a new life in England and, we hoped, be reunited with Zofia, Helcia and Józef. Perhaps the political climate would change in Poland. And if I were too old by then, maybe my grandchildren, if there were any, would pay their respects on my behalf, visit all the graves.

Other Countries

Waking up   to the world

     destroyed   not completely

     the trees pulled   sleeping [thus]   to wake

and blur   waiting   for things to grow again

voices coaxing   a viewpoint

    temporal point to cut the sector into segment

folded up ruler in pocket

    a stone to drown

               Say *the night sorry*
             say *the lullaby broken*
             into separate sound   say
             awake now say *together* say *starbeam*
             main beam dooryard frame
             say *another*   say *stay* or say *nothing*

After the chapter ends

the new chasm   step   away from

and drown   [remembrance]

nine kilometers of days

that will not stay apart

keep to their sides   of the fences

[those] strange canvasses blooming amorphous

       surfaces *of* _____

are not true   shut [them] away

Coaxed   down   [such] infinitude
           just the road there   and its oiled pages

songs of impossible homecoming   agony

        's   uncontrollable   bend[s]

The ear sung back   to the flayed spine

To finally arrive   detached   everything changed

a disposition distended   skipping in a new coat

with shiny buttons   *Go to work*

let the children play hide-and-seek in the attic

but do not let them wander   beyond the shed

New beginnings

CHAPTER 8

Other Countries (*Zofia*)

Africa, England, U.S.A., 1948–1955

OUR DREAMS of the new Poland, led by our military that had been fighting in North Africa and Italy (and training in Palestine)—forsaken. There was nothing to return to where our farm had once been; the Polish government-in-exile betrayed by sharp pens that signed new agreements in the Tehran and Yalta conferences and recarved Poland's borders. The smaller version that emerged after the end of the War was not really Poland but a country led by a panoply of superimposed Russian indoctrinates who pulled the strings, made the puppets think they were at the center of the subtly shrinking stage.

Would our family of five be reunited, reassembled into an awkward star? Margin-arcs between us, deep moats where we each wandered absentmindedly, uncontrollably in sleep's uncertain hours. Perpetually shredding the worn pages of our memories that would somehow find shape again. Helcia's trail of ripped papers folded and refolded.

The haunting of the past, the blurring of color and shape. Just colors on a map, lines and curves on a document that can be unrolled and pointed to thus:

Ours now. The rightful heirs.

We were transported with the other Polish women and children from Tanganyika in massive military trucks to Nairobi, Kenya. I studied the landscape carefully on that route, knowing I would never see Africa again. Its open landscape, sprawling skies, and wild animals. Nor Poland. Our beautiful orchards, our farm, our home. I wanted to weep but could not. Józef and Helcia dozed near me. I, too, was incredibly tired yet unable to sleep.

In Nairobi we visited the Red Cross office and learned that they had located Andrzej and Henryk; a telegram had been sent to instruct them to meet us in London, England. It was difficult to believe but was confirmed with smiles and nods. We were numb on the plane, reeling from the good news.

From Nairobi we flew to London. Our first plane ride. Józef was excited to be seemingly a thousand miles elevated in the air. Helcia and I remained lost somewhere on the ground. I still thought of Józef as my baby, but he was twelve, the age of Henryk when we were deported from Poland. All three of us were sick though used to not feeling well over the last eight years. Perhaps the flight contributed.

When the plane finally landed, we looked for Andrzej and Henryk eagerly, but they weren't there. We hadn't seen Henryk since a few weeks after he joined the Young Polish Battalion in 1942 and Andrzej since he left Siberia in 1941. The message from the Red Cross probably hadn't reached them yet.

We were transported to a civilian camp, Lilford, in Northamptonshire, a few hours' train ride north of London. We rode in a passenger train and not cattle cars this time, thankfully. Helcia, Józef and I were anxious to be reunited with Andrzej and Henryk. I worried about how much they had changed after the years of hardship and war, and also how we would appear to them.

Several depressing weeks passed at the civilian camp. The barracks were very rudimentary and the weather, cold. Our levels of hopefulness waned each day. Perhaps the Red Cross hadn't found them. Perhaps there was some kind of mix-up and they weren't alive. Helcia wrote additional letters to the Red Cross inquiring about Andrzej and Henryk, notifying them again that we waited at Camp Lilford. It seemed impossible for us to figure our future without them.

Andrzej and Henryk finally located us in our camp a few weeks later. My husband and oldest son both looked older. Henryk, clearly a man now, had put on some much-needed weight. Andrzej had aged, as to be expected, as we all had, I was sure. It was difficult to believe the size of the scar on the left side of his face. As much as I tried not to look at the traces of his wound, I was drawn to the lines, to the history permanently etched on his skin. We were lucky that he was alive. That we had all survived. So many others had not.

It took several hours for us to catch up, to narrate the events after our paths had splintered into different trajectories. Andrzej and Henryk had boarded separate ships from Alexandria, Egypt to the port of Southampton in southern England, and had been assigned to different military camps. The words blurred; I wasn't even sure what was said. I continued staring at Andrzej's scar, at the smaller seams that strayed from the main scar. For quite some time, I remained lost somewhere in the map of his injury and couldn't find my way out to hear the conversation of my children and husband humming in the background. Again, I was struck with the possibility that I was dreaming a pleasant dream in my sleep at the camp, but each time I blinked, my husband and oldest son were still with us, in yet another country.

Andrzej and Henryk returned to their respective military camps; Andrzej to Surrey, Henryk back to Scotland. Henryk had signed up for a deep-sea fishing course, one of the options offered to transition the young military into civilian life. It was a six-month course in Aberdeen, Scotland that culminated in a two-week fishing expedition in the North Sea. After completing the intensive course and excursion, Henryk would be a full-fledged deep-sea fisherman. I had a feeling this career choice resulted as a practical compromise for him; choices remained limited at this juncture, but I was happy he had a direction, a plan, something on which to focus.

I believe we all slept more soundly that night than in a very long time. There seemed to be a flicker of optimism again beyond the overwhelming stasis.

Polish veterans and civilians who had nowhere to go over-crowded the military and civilian camps in England. There were no specific plans yet for any of us. Helcia, Józef and I remained in the civilian camp in Lilford for weeks with nothing to do, not knowing the next steps forward. Helcia and Józef grew increasingly restless from pure boredom. Gradually they started exploring nearby towns and villages, looking for bread to bring back. I was happy to know the exact whereabouts of Andrzej and Henryk after seven years of separation but was overwhelmed with anxiety about our future. There were days I could hardly even get up but forced myself to do so for Helcia and Józef, so they wouldn't have the extra burden of worrying about me. I lacked the industriousness I had had in Siberia and Tanganyika, the urge to create a sense of home life, a daily routine.

After several months the British authorities created the Polish Army Resettlement Corps for the sole purpose of transitioning Polish soldiers back into civilian life. There were not enough jobs for discharged British soldiers, let alone Poles. Few options existed for the Poles in England: working underground in the coal mines in Wales, helping in the forestry industry (which Andrzej and Henryk had had enough of) in northern England, washing dishes in a hotel restaurant or café, or working in the building industry as a laborer to reconstruct England's housing stock after the devastation of bombing during the War.

The Polish Army Resettlement Corps granted each family one scholarship for college. Since Henryk was eligible for assistance from the Polish Cadet Corps and was enrolled in the deep-sea fishermen program in Scotland, Andrzej and I urged Helcia to apply for the scholarship. She indicated she wanted to attend Tooting College's business school in south London. When she applied in person for the scholarship, the two people in the office scrutinized her grades and informed her that she qualified for a four-year degree in Dublin, where many other college-prepared Poles had applied for various programs. One of Henryk's fellow cadets was accepted into medical school in Dublin to become an ophthalmologist.

Helcia explained to the two kind people in the scholarship office that she would like to attend Tooting College. She wasn't feeling well and didn't believe she could handle the four-year program. She was chronically fatigued. It had been difficult to remember things when she was teaching in Tanganyika. My daughter would go to business school, which would also expedite her full-time employment and shorten the length of her studies.

Henryk returned very disheartened from his excursion in the North Sea. He requested a transfer to a camp near London, attesting that the two weeks fishing in the North Sea comprised the most horrible experience of his life, worse than Siberia. It was bitterly cold, the sea was rough, everybody was seasick the entire time; no one could keep food down. While gutting the fish, which was part of the job, it was impossible to distinguish the fish from one's own frozen hands. I was glad he was back in England with us for now and would seek a career on land.

Daily life in the camps became increasingly bleak. The camps hadn't been designed as permanent shelter, just a "holding tank" while we decided where we would live, what country we could belong to. Our Polish citizenship was stripped from us since we refused to go back to Poland under Soviet rule.

Helcia left our camp to stay in London with a classmate, also named Helcia, from Tengeru. Henryk soon followed since the city provided more opportunities. He secured a job as a hotel porter on Oxford Street and later became a floor waiter in the Grosvenor Hotel over Victoria train station. He and Helcia rented an apartment large enough to bring Andrzej, Józef and me to live with them. In a strange reversal of roles, they had become the parents. It was difficult to fathom that they were adults, but their actions and behavior proved such, and I was silently grateful. They knew, I felt sure.

Andrzej found a job in a biscuit factory in south London. Over two hundred Polish workers were employed there, including three generals and eight colonels. They all reported to a supervisor who had been a corporal but spoke English fluently, unlike the high-ranking officers. The children's English was good because of the intense classes after deportation; Andrzej's and mine, unfortunately, non-existent. After a couple of years we saved enough money to purchase a small house near

Brixton in south London. The house had to be purchased in Henryk's name since Andrzej was too old to qualify for a mortgage.

Helcia worked as a "finisher" while attending classes at Tooting; she was responsible for the final handwork for a seamstress—sewing on buttons, hemming, taking care of any final alterations that needed to be done by hand. Józef attended a high school near London that was more like a trade school where he studied drafting.

After Helcia finished her business program, she worked in London for a patent bureau, Mathys and Squire. A friend of hers from one of her classes had referred her. They were looking for someone with some experience but someone they didn't have to compensate too highly. Helcia was given the job and the salary was acceptable to her. She was responsible for typing and retyping patents, transcribing handwriting with a dictionary next to her, nervous about her English skills, which everyone thought were excellent. She met Czesław, her friend's brother, at a family gathering she was invited to. She had actually met Czesław briefly in the civilian camp when he came to visit someone who had been with his group of deportees in Uzbekistan. Czesław had been in the Royal Air Force during the War after his family had been deported to Siberia in the first wave, like us. His older brother was killed in Poland on the last day of the War while serving in the Polish army under General Berling, fighting alongside the Red Army, and was buried in northern Poland.

Helcia and Czesław married that August; her friend Helcia from Tengeru became her sister-in-law. It was difficult to fathom that my oldest was twenty-five years old and a married woman. I felt robbed of many years with my children in Poland. I had no idea how extraordinary those days on our farm had been. If only to go back and savor them better this time, memorize everything I had taken for granted back then, how the wind felt through the orchard trees, how the sunlight illuminated the children's eyes.

England became crowded with many like us, stranded by the War without a home to return to. Jobs grew scarcer as time went by; the prospects for our future looked increasingly austere. British trade unions and the general public were becoming more openly hostile toward us, the Polish "refugees" that competed for jobs, housing, and dwindling resources. The British newspapers and speeches by socialist Members of Parliament in the House of Commons accentuated this antagonism. The trade union movement leadership depended on financial assistance from the Soviet Union, which intensified the propaganda against Polish exiles.

In addition to the anti-Polish sentiment, the pace in London was very fast and we all wanted to rest. Some families we knew were going to Canada, Argentina and Brazil to begin new lives.

Right around that time (1951), the American Congress granted forty thousand additional visas to displaced Poles who had served actively in the military. Andrzej convinced me that there would be more prospects for Henryk, Helcia and Józef in the United States. I didn't want to go. I was tired of new countries, too old to learn English. He promised this would be our final country of residence; we were both resigned to the fact that we would never return to Poland. As veterans of the military, Andrzej and Henryk both qualified for the additional visas granted by the American Congress, and without wasting any time, applied quickly.

Each received three tickets. Czesław and Helcia, at first, remained undecided about the United States. Czesław's parents and sister planned to stay in London in Herne Hill, near

Brixton. I'm sure Helcia convinced her husband to try life in America. I was ecstatic. I told her to choose where her husband wanted to live, but with my entire being prayed they would move to the United States. There was a bond between my daughter and me after all we had endured the last twelve years that I could not bear to relinquish.

The day after New Year's 1952, Andrzej, Józef and I boarded a ship destined for New York City. Helcia, Czesław and Henryk had been issued tickets on a different ship, the *Olympia*, to Halifax, Canada. They would take the train from Canada and meet us in New York at Andrzej's sister's apartment. Andrzej's sister Wiktusia was living on St. Mark's Place in lower Manhattan and invited us to stay with her as long as we needed a place.

Because it was winter in the Atlantic, both ship rides were tumultuous and cold. It took seven days to finally glimpse the Statue of Liberty and reach the harbor of New York City. The thick fog that enveloped the Statue and her harbor made the end of the journey seem very tenuous. Instead of a torch, the Statue of Liberty appeared to have the whole world pressing down on her, extinguishing the light of freedom. I reminded myself that thousands of immigrants had passed this same way earlier in the century in search of better lives.

It took Henryk, Helcia and Czesław eight days to reach Halifax, Canada from Southampton, a trip that normally takes five days. As a result of seasickness and the inability to retain any food, Henryk was too dehydrated and physically weakened to remember going through customs in St. John's and the train ride with Helcia and Czesław to New York City.

We all stayed with Wiktusia for about two weeks. Andrzej hadn't seen his sister since 1929 when she had left Poland. They reminisced about their childhood and narrated the events since they had last seen each other. Andrzej did not delve into much detail; I don't think he had the energy to unearth everything we had experienced and convey those details to another, especially close family. Not now and maybe never. The shrapnel still lodged in his head prevented doing so. It was better to suppress those recollections than risk prompting a landslide.

New York was not as I had imagined it. I felt claustrophobic, especially after the years of open, wild spaces in Tanganyika. I kept thinking that the tall buildings might fall—and was deathly afraid to walk under them.

Czesław and Helcia found an apartment in Brooklyn rather quickly and moved first. Helcia secured an administrative job in Petro-Chem on 42nd Street in New York City. Czesław soon found work sending photo plates from the United States to Encylopedia Britannica's London office. Andrzej, Henryk and I boarded a train to Hartford, Connecticut to stay with Andrzej's brother, Janek, at 44 Barber Street, Windsor, Conn.—the address we had all memorized in 1940. We lived with him for a few weeks until we bought a house nearby on Colton Street. It was a two-bedroom house with a modest yard, much smaller than our home and property in Piłsudczyzna, yet luxurious in contrast to all of our provisional living situations since.

In September 1952, just as we were starting to feel settled in Connecticut, the name of which I still couldn't pronounce, a formal letter arrived for Henryk informing him that he was drafted into the United States Army to serve in the Korean War. The document didn't appear to have the same effect on him as it did on Andrzej and me. I wasn't sure if I could live through another war that involved one of my children.

Henryk was stationed at Fort Dix, New Jersey, from 1952 to 1954 and placed in charge of a weapons pool. He issued rifles to new recruits taking basic training, instructed them on weapon maintenance, and drew their ammunition for the practice range. In anticipation of deployment to Korea, he and other non-American soldiers applied for American citizenship. Henryk, like all of us, had lost his Polish citizenship by refusing to repatriate to Poland after the War. Should he be sent to Korea and become a prisoner of war without being a legal citizen of any country, he would not be protected by the Geneva Conventions. Thankfully, he was never deployed to Korea, as the war ended.

After his discharge from the army in 1954, he found a job delivering furniture. Three weeks into the job, a Polish woman who was moving with her two sisters, pulled him aside and advised in all seriousness "this job will kill you." He was far too thin and his coloring did not look good to her either, she told him. On a piece of paper she wrote down the name of a Polish man she knew who worked in one of the major insurance companies in Hartford, Connecticut.

"Call him. Go meet with him," she instructed. "He'll find you a better job, so that you don't die doing this after everything you've been through."

Henryk met with the Polish man referred to him, who informed him that in all honesty, he wasn't qualified for anything in his payroll auditing department, but that he could start out in the mailroom and work his way up, especially with some school. Henryk enrolled in evening classes at Hillyer College (which later merged with two other small colleges to become the University of Hartford) in January of 1955 on the G.I. Bill while working full-time at Aetna Insurance Company; first in the mailroom, then in filing, then in the accounting and actuarial departments.

Józef attended drafting school full time. Andrzej found

work in a factory, and I cleaned offices in Hartford at night. Often while cleaning the empty rooms, I drifted back to Poland, to the cattle cars, the barracks in Siberia, the clay hut in Uzbekistan, the mud huts of Africa, the civilian camps of England—I would catch myself and become surprised again that I was in the United States. Helcia and Czesław would be moving to Connecticut that November to begin their family and to be close to us.

It was difficult, but miraculous, to believe that we would all be together again. At last.

Coda

Henryk

The Burial (*Henryk*)

Windsor, Connecticut, U.S.A., 1955

THE RESIDENTS of Connecticut complained that winter that it was bitterly cold, but it seemed mild to my family compared to our two winters in Siberia and the raw, rainy winters in London. The freezing long days and dark hours in the taiga revisited our memories; the forty-below-zero windchill tearing at our faces, fingers and toes. Spitting ice, walking in ripped shoes without a country. Trudging over an hour and back to fell colossal trees.

The ground was beginning to thaw that particular winter on Colton Street when I dug a medium-sized grave approximately three feet deep. Hovering in the windows of our house that we had purchased for $5,400 (in my name since my father was too old in this country, also, to be considered for a mortgage), my father and mother watched me. They were a peculiar presence half-hiding behind the curtains Helcia had sewed for us—quiet witnesses that made the moment seem factual, an actual occurrence, not merely a singular journey in one's dark labyrinth of thoughts.

My brother must have been inside at the kitchen table busy with drafting school work. Tata had returned from working at the Cushman chuck factory. Józef and I translated for him and Mother regularly. They felt too old to learn a new language; they reiterated that they were tired. Helcia was most likely preparing dinner for her husband Czesław and herself in Brooklyn. They planned to move to Connecticut in a few months. They longed for a slower pace, too—more trees, more sky.

The "grave" in our backyard was ready. I could find no other resting place for the metal box containing two hundred and fifty rounds of belt ammunition we used to fire Browning Automatic Rifles that I had forgotten about after my discharge from the United States Army. I had been in charge of the ammunition depot and weapons pool at Fort Dix and had a small stash in the trunk of my car, everything short of bazookas: grenades, night goggles, clips of bullets that I would give to Wujek Janek who, working in New York City, always carried his .38 caliber revolver. It seemed perfectly appropriate to bury the dangerous loot underground during winter so that by spring we would all have forgotten, or so I wished—as I shoveled the earth over my last tangible connection to war.

A few months earlier in New York, I had met a Polish-American young woman, Irene Jarosz, who was marching in traditional Polish costume at the Pułaski parade. I didn't want her to get the wrong impression if she happened to see these last vestiges of war in my trunk. Her parents had emigrated to the United States in the 1920s through Ellis Island; Irene spoke Polish fluently and could communicate with my parents. I was ready to establish roots to cultivate somewhere permanently.

Years would pass, drawing circles around us like the enormous circumferences of the trees in the Arctic forest. My father would continue working in the Cushman chuck factory until his sudden heart attack in 1962. Five out of nine of his grandchildren met him. Mama lived with Helcia until her own death in 1986. She spent a great deal of her time listening to

Polish radio programs, knew very little English, and fought against the pacemaker she needed.

My siblings and I remained slightly estranged—from the gaps of geography and time, the harshness of what we had suffered, and the silence that suffering had ingrained. We would stay in the same town, tucked into our houses with our spouses and our children, who would never completely understand. We would come to offer them magic keys—educations and chances to surpass us; look backwards and say "teach us to be selfless like you were. To offer our children even more." Some of my father's grandchildren would visit our ancestors' graves, I was sure, and perhaps even reassemble the story my parents could not tell.

Though no longer on the farm, we still toiled for our labor—in blue and white collar, to save for the unknown. Not to waste but to give because there was meager abundance. It was enough for us to go to work and come home not in the cold, without the impending threat of court-martial or withheld food rations, with a regular paycheck that enabled us to eat, save, and rest with our family to rise the next day. We would never forget the blood shed for nations, the hours of dread and then—when the green buds unfolded eternal spring—our continual survival.

Then we said "enough," the command to forget, to carve out a passage, a room to walk through. For reaching the ends of our days with our loved ones and our private reconciliations with history. Our own sense of wealth balanced by loss.

BIBLIOGRAPHY

Bibliography

Maps and Shadows is a novel that is based on historical fact. It is the history of my father and his family—a history shared by almost 1.5 million other Poles who were deported to Siberia by Stalin.

For those readers who might want to delve more into the history underlying *Maps and Shadows*, I am including this partial bibliography of books that informed my own research.

Adamczyk, Wesley. *When God Looked the Other Way: An Odyssey of War, Exile, and Redemption*. Chicago: University of Chicago Press, 2004.

Anders, Władysław. *An Army in Exile: The Story of the Second Polish Corps*. Nashville, TN: Battery Press, 2004.

Barabasz, Edward G. *As I Remember*. New York: Carlton Press, 1974.

Blumenson, Martin. *Bloody River: The Real Tragedy of the Rapido*. College Station, TX: Texas A&M University Press, 1998.

Davies, Norman. *God's Playground: A History of Poland. Vol.2: 1795 to the Present*. New York: Columbia University Press, 2005.

Gillon, Adam, Ludwik Krzyżanowski, and Krystyna Olszer. *Introduction to Modern Polish Literature: An Anthology of Fiction and Poetry*. New York: Hippocrene, 1982.

Hautzig, Esther. *The Endless Steppe: Growing Up in Siberia.* New York: Harper Trophy, 1987.

Hempel, Andrew. *Poland in World War II: An Illustrated Military History.* New York: Hippocrene, 2005.

Higginbotham, Jay. *Fast Train Russia.* New York: Dodd, Mead, 1983.

Kawecka, Zdzisława Krystyna. *Journey Without a Ticket: To England through Siberia.* Nottingham, England: Z.K. Kawecka, 1988.

Konarski, Feliks. *Czerwone maki na Monte Cassino: wiersze i piosenki, 1939–1945* (The Red Poppies on Monte Cassino. Poems and Songs, 1939–1945). Warsaw, Poland: LTW, 2004.

Krolikowski, Lucjan. *Stolen Childhood: A Saga of Polish War Children.* Trans. Kazimierz J. Rozniatowski. Buffalo, NY: Father Justin Rosary Hour, 1983.

Madeja, Witold. *The Polish 2nd Corps and the Italian Campaign, 1943–1945.* Allentown, PA: Valor and Game Publishing, 1984.

Miłosz, Czesław. *The History of Polish Literature.* Berkeley: University of California Press, 1983.

Olson, Lynne, and Stanley Cloud. *A Question of Honor: The Kościuszko Squadron: Forgotten Heroes of World War II.* New York: Vintage, 2004.

Parker, Matthew. *Monte Cassino: The Hardest-Fought Battle of World War II.* New York: Anchor Books, 2005.

Piotrowski, Tadeusz, ed. *The Polish Deportees of World War II: Recollections of Removal to the Soviet Union and Dispersal Throughout the World.* Jefferson, NC: McFarland, 2004.

——.*Vengeance of the Swallows: Memoir of a Polish Family's Ordeal Under Soviet Aggression, Ukrainian Ethnic Cleansing And Nazi Enslavement, and Their Emigration to America.* Jefferson, NC: McFarland, 1995.

Rumi, Jalalu'l-Din. *Rumi: Poet and Mystic*. Trans. Reynold A. Nicholson. London, England: Mandala Books, 1978.

Solzhenitsyn, Aleksandr I. *The Gulag Archipelago 1918–1956: An Experiment in Literary Investigation*. Trans. Thomas P. Whitney and Harry Willetts. Abridged by Edward E. Ericson, Jr. New York: Harper Perennial, 2002.

Wiesel, Elie. *Night*. Trans. Marion Wiesel. New York: Hill and Wang, 2006.

ACKNOWLEDGEMENTS

Józef, Helcia and Henryk - 2010

Acknowledgements

I thank my father Henry first, for talking about his experiences, answering scores of questions, writing down facts, and tirelessly rereading draft versions. Secondly, my Ciocia (Aunt) Helen for sending me to various books years ago, and over the past few years, for traveling back in her memory to narrate painful events and to review my words for accuracy.

I am most appreciative of the input I received from my first readers, Amanda Herbert, Jadwiga (Hedy) Wasner, Ori Hawkins, Judy Zawadski, Jennifer Sutherland, Tom Boido, Denise Rodriguez, Keith Dahlke and Keith Gregory. There have been many mentors over the years: David Leeming, Marilyn Nelson, Joan Joffe Hall, Gina Barreca and Ann Lauterbach. I honor the memory of teachers and friends who have passed away: Maxine Johnson, Mary Ellen Messina, Ed Rivera, Kameron Wade.

Lastly, I thank both my parents for the strong sense of family and love they have given selflessly since the day they brought me home, as well as the many years of education they have provided for me. I realize how extraordinarily fortunate I am to have been granted such opportunities.

KRYSIA JOPEK

May 2010
WINDSOR, CONNECTICUT

READING GROUP GUIDE

Reading Group Guide

1. Author Krysia Jopek divides the narration of her story among four different points of view: Henryk, the brother; Helcia, the sister; Zofia, the mother; and Andrzej, the father. Why do you think she may have chosen this approach?

2. How are the coming events foreshadowed in the description of the idyllic life on the family farm?

3. Henryk describes his *osada* or village as "an oasis surrounded by Ukrainian villages." What is the significance of this geography for Henryk and his family?

4. What reasons do the Russian soldiers give for the family's sudden deportation? In spite of their deportation, why does the family consider itself lucky?

5. Helcia expresses her fear of the unknown future by scribbling on bits of paper torn from her precious dictionary. What's the significance of this and why do you think she compares her actions to those who stuff messages into the Wailing Wall?

6. Despite the deprivations of their Siberian labor camp, Zofia manages to get one or two pints of milk a week for Józef, the youngest child. How does she do it? And why does she say that

the boy was, among the three children, either "the luckiest or perhaps, the most scarred" by the experience?

7. Poetry can illuminate a subject in a very different way than prose. How does the poetry in *Maps and Shadows* add to the reading experience?

8. Why does Helcia call "44 Barber Street, Windsor, Conn." a "rectangular flag of hope"?

9. The upheavals experienced by individuals and families as the result of history is a theme of *Maps and Shadows*. What historic events caused the family to leave their home in Poland, and subsequently to leave Siberia? Has anyone in your family experienced similar upheavals?

10. When the Polish forced laborers are freed by the Russians, why does Andrzej decide it's best to leave his family and join the Polish Army?

11. After nearly two years in Siberia, Zofia, Helcia and her youngest brother, Józef, arrive in Tanganyika. How does the author convey the atmosphere in Africa?

12. Freed at last from the frozen forests of Siberia, fourteen-year-old Henryk finds himself in the desert of the Middle East as a member of the Young Polish Battalion. In what ways is this geographically hostile setting a metaphor for Henryk's life?

13. During the emotionally charged scene when Henryk and his father are reunited in Gaza, the boy observes that his tata has changed. But, he thinks, so has he. Discuss the universal and often conflicting feelings that arise whenever a parent and child reunite after a period of time.

14. Zofia finally arrives at the refugee camp in England, closer than ever to reuniting with her husband and son. Yet she says she's lost all the energy she had in Siberia. Why do you think this happened?

15. Looking back on her life, Zofia observes that she didn't properly appreciate the years the family lived on their beautiful farm in Poland. Do we all tend to only really appreciate our blessings when they're gone? Is there a lesson here?

16. Why does the family—along with so many of their compatriots—refuse to return to Poland after the War?

17. What happens to Helcia's treasured dictionary? What does its fate say about Helcia's dreams of teaching?

18. What are the lasting effects of the family's exile from Poland on each of the book's four characters? How does that experience continue to resonate beyond the generation that experienced it?

19. Discuss the significance of the burial at the book's end.

ABOUT THE AUTHOR

 **KRYSIA JOPEK**, a multi-published poet, received her B.A. and M.A. in English from the University of Connecticut, her M.Phil. in English from the City University of New York (CUNY) Graduate Center, and her M.F.A in Literary Fiction from Albertus Magnus. She studied in London, England for a year, and taught English literature and writing at City College of New York for ten years, and subsequently taught English at Westfield State University. She currently resides in Connecticut.

Jopek brings her rich literary and poetic background, and a worldview of global dimension, to illuminate a lost piece of World War II history with lyricism and grace.